On your deathbed, will you have joy and contentment with the type of life you have chosen to live today?

Life revolves around others, and without them has virtually no meaning; yet life is also a single player game. On our deathbed, we are the ones who have to live with the choices we've made.

It's never too late to live the life you know in your gut you are supposed to live.

It's never too late to make the little or big choices to become the person you know you were meant to become.

It's never too late.

The best time was many years ago, the second best time is now.

We only get one life, Isn't it time we start to live like it?

Love,
JMM

i

Finish Empty

Joshua Medcalf

Contents

CHAPTER 1

"Do I look scared?"

Budapest, Hungary. The Past.

Sweat dripped down the masked man's face, making it difficult for him to see. He blinked it away, shouting even louder this time: "Put it in the bag! Everything, NOW!!!"

Behind the counter, a terrified older woman stared back at him, shaking and frozen with fear.

The man gestured roughly with his 9mm Beretta pistol. "I said put it in the bag!" As he jabbed the barrel toward her, she obeyed. Reaching down, her wrinkled and trembling hands pulled cash from the register. The gunman flipped through the thin stack, angry. "That's it?!"

She nodded, terrified. "I'm sorry. It's all we have."

The gunman stuffed it into his jacket, then turned around. Behind him, another gunman covered the rest of the room with his own pistol.

It was a small family diner, the kind built up from nothing by long hours and loving care from the people who owned it. But right now, the air was thick with fear. A dozen customers sat frozen, eyes locked on the men or crying with their eyes on the floor.

The gunman at the register gestured angrily around the room. "Everyone empty your pockets! Wallets, purses. Cash on the table! Now!" The patrons rushed to obey. Frantic. Panicking, driven by fear.

All except for one man.

A young Japanese man in his early twenties sat alone in the corner, calmly eating his meal. Head in the newspaper, he was completely unbothered by everything happening around him.

The second gunman noticed, approaching him aggressively. "Hey, you! Everything that's in your wallet! Put it on the table, now!"

The young man looked up at the gunman and calmly replied, "Wrong guy."

The gunman blinked in surprise. *Who did this man think he was?* He was unarmed! He was small in stature. "Do you want to get yourself killed!?"

The young man took his napkin from his lap and calmly brushed crumbs from his face, *then* he stood up. He was much shorter than the gunman, but his intensity and conviction held a kind of power that a gun couldn't match. He stared the gunman directly in the eye. The gunman blinked, instinctively stepping back, startled by the small man's presence. He silently wondered if he was concealing a weapon on his body.

Staring directly and deeply into the gunman's eyes, he was almost smirking as he said, "Let me ask you a question. Do I look scared?"

Behind his mask, the gunman froze, thrown. He didn't know what to do.

The smaller man continued, "You, on the other hand... your heart rate is well above 170 beats per minute, and your pupils indicate the drugs in your body are overloading your nervous system with cortisol and spiking your adrenaline. Despite the fact that it's quite chilly in this room, you're sweating like you've just run from a bear. In fact, I'd say you're not far away from blacking out." He smirked, a targeted edge of condescension in his tone.

"First time?" The question phrased like a statement, hit the gunman's fragile ego snapping him out of the trance.

But it was too late.

As he tried to pull the trigger, the smaller man was already a fluid blur of motion. Catching the pistol barrel, he knocked it towards the ceiling as the gun fired. Then an excruciating pain the gunman had never felt before exploded across his nervous system as his elbow shattered. *That arm would never be the same.* The gun fell and — as the shock started to hit — the smaller man struck him sharply in the throat. Gasping and breathless, the robber fell to the floor seething in pain.

Nearby, the first gunman stood frozen by what he'd just witnessed. Before he could blink, the smaller man kicked the table violently into his hip with an explosion of graceful motion like that of an assassin.

Just as the downed gunman got free of the table, the man leveled a kick to the side of his knee that was so precise you could hear the tendons snap from a hundred meters away. The gun fell from his hand as he collapsed to the ground.

Calm and cool as the backside of a pillow, the smaller man picked up the weapons, disassembling them in seconds. He handed them over to the elderly woman at the register, who couldn't help but let out a small smile.

Only she knew who he was.
Only she knew his name: <u>Akira</u>.

He handed her three crisp bills, apologetic. "I'm sorry for the mess, Okasan. I didn't mean to cause any trouble. It's best I'm not here when the police arrive."

She beamed with gratitude. "I can't thank you enough." She wasn't his biological mother, but she had taken him in like a son many years ago.

As he walked out of the restaurant, one of the awestruck customers approached the woman and stuttered. "Whooooo was that guy?"

Okasan just smiled.

Only she knew that Akira was born and molded in the dark.

No one knew much about his past, because he revealed so little about it. All she knew was that it was very rough. Orphaned at a young age, he lived on the streets until he was discovered by a man that Akira said had changed his life, transforming his pain into a powerful force of energy and skills.

*That is how he could laugh at things others found dangerous —
whatever had happened in his past, and whatever training he had been through, it had taught him powerful lessons.*

He was not afraid of death.
Akira was liberated by it.
He meditated on death every day.
It was through this practice that he was ironically able to be fully present and fully alive.

Because above all, he knew that the purpose of life was not to arrive safely at death.

But Okasan wasn't in the practice of telling other people's secrets. So instead, she just beamed with the pride of a mother. "You'll find out someday. Everyone will."

* * *

Tokyo, Japan. The Present.

"Akira? Akira?! AKIRA—"

With a blink, that same small man — now many decades older, but with the same unmistakable calm presence — slowly stretched his arms and legs from the nap he had been enjoying.

Akira was in a doctor's office, as a nurse gently woke him up. "Mr. Akira, how are you doing?"

He wiped a bit of drool from the corner of his mouth and smiled. "I'm fine. Sorry about that, I must have dozed off."

"You definitely did. You know, if you weren't so cute, we would have a problem!"

She winked at him, and Akira just grinned back. "We wouldn't want that, would we?"

She smiled. "The doctor will be in any minute. He has *the results.*"

Akira nodded as the air was sucked out of the room. Both of them had a pretty good idea what those results would show.

CHAPTER 2

The Slopes

Aspen, Colorado.

Icy wind cut across the mountaintop as a small figure coasted toward the massive halfpipe, a bright white plume of snow spitting from her snowboard.

Nakoma was only 13 years old, but she rode like a pro.

In fact, she would try out for the US National Team in six months — and that was more of a formality than anything else. Everyone said she was destined for greatness, but that was before the incident. Now it felt like all anyone wanted to talk about was the incident.

Before that day, they had said she was the Tiger Woods of snowboarding. And for good reason, too — at 6 years old, and without telling anyone, she took a hard right turn for a 12-foot jump, and effortlessly threw a backflip she had seen much older riders do thousands of times. She had been obsessed with the trick as a baby. Any time she was crying, her parents would put on a video of a backflip Shaun White once threw in the Olympics, and she would smile and instantly be pacified, sometimes watching it on repeat for hours.

But this morning, her mind was locked on the trick she was about to attempt. She was preparing it for the Winter X Games, where she would be competing in 8 weeks. Her new coach had choreographed her run, and told her that in order to place, she needed to land this — a backside 900, one of the most difficult tricks in snowboarding. Up until this year, Nakoma never had choreographed her runs. She just threw tricks as they came to her, but the new coach had told her "that doesn't work at this level."

As she gained speed, the world seemed to blur, narrowing to just her and the halfpipe. She dropped into the pipe, rocketing down its U-shaped curve and popping up into the air on the other side. She hung there for a second, seeming to float suspended, before dropping back in. Gathering momentum, she hit the opposite side and shot skyward again, twisting into the backside rotation.

The world turned upside down — once, twice — hurtling towards the magical two-and-a-half spins. For a moment, Nakoma hung there, defying gravity — before her patented soft as a bird landing on the hard-packed snow. But as she landed, the lip of her board caught an edge, throwing her off-balance. With a wobble, she wiped out hard.

A man's voice called from just up the slope. "Nakoma! Are you okay?"

She slowly popped to her feet, after a quick scream of frustration. "Yeah. I'm fine, Dad. I *LOVE* wiping out *AFTER* I've completed the hard part of a trick!!"

Her father coasted down the slope and eased to a stop nearby, pulling his goggles up.

Jonathan's face was lined with a few extra wrinkles now, marking the years that had passed after he'd left Japan. Since then, life had taken him around the world, to the top of his profession — and twice, to the top of an Olympic podium. Akira had trained him well, and his pursuit of mastery in archery had paid off with countless wins, brand deals, and

7

now, a thriving business in the consulting industry that was built off his name and reputation.

But the thing he cared about most was right here in front of him.

Nakoma's beauty and intuition were gifts from her mother, but that relentless and sometimes reckless competitive fire was all Jonathan. They shared a love for athletics, and spent countless hours together training on the slopes, and competing in everything from silly card games, to archery, to workouts. Jonathan's experience as a professional athlete, complete with the tools he'd learned long ago from his sensei Akira, were a huge competitive advantage for Nakoma.

But like Jonathan had learned years earlier, success is a long journey, requiring steadfast faithfulness to the daily practice of chopping wood and carrying water. More than anything, it's *a willingness to endure*. To endure boredom, the mundane, and all the trials and tribulations along the bumpy, winding roads in the dark that allow you to look talented and effortless under the bright lights.

Today, that meant another wipeout, the ninth in a row. Try as she might, Nakoma couldn't seem to land the trick.

Jonathan read her frustration, and immediately knew what was behind it. There was a lot more going on in his daughter's mind than pulling off a backside 900, and he guessed that she needed the space to deal with it on her own time.

"Do you want to talk about it?"

She shook her head. "No. I DO NOT want to talk about it."

Jonathan nodded, gently. "Just thought I'd ask. And remember, anything that h—"

"Anything that happens to me today is in my best interest and an opportunity to learn and grow," Nakoma finished his words with the kind of sass that only teenage girls have perfected. She knew the phrase by heart, thanks to Jonathan searing it into her heart and mind from the time she was born, and she knew the power in it. But today, she didn't want to hear it. She didn't want to hear *anything*.

Jonathan's phone rang. It was the lodge manager: "Jonathan? You should get down here. There's two people in suits asking to see you immediately." His voice dropped to a whisper, "These guys look like Feds or CIA, it seems serious."

Jonathan thanked him and hung up. While it wasn't abnormal for his phone to be ringing off the hook, even on a weekend like this, it was strange to have someone actually show up at the mountain to see him. As he and Nakoma headed back down, he couldn't help but wonder what it was all about.

* * *

As Jonathan and Nakoma got close to the *Dancing Bear*, where they always stayed when training in Aspen, indeed there were two bulky men in dark suits and shades waiting outside a black Chevy Suburban that appeared military grade.

The first man seemed to recognize Jonathan immediately, "Jonathan, we are colleagues of an old friend of yours, Mr. Akira. He has requested that we pick you up and bring you to him."

Jonathan smiled, feeling much better that it was just Akira doing weird Akira things, "He's here? He didn't have to send you guys. He could have just called."

The man in the suit shook his head. "No sir, he's still at home. That's where he'd like you to join him."

"In Japan?" Confused at this strange request, Jonathan thought through his options. "Okay, I'm sure I can speak with my assistant and carve out some time over the next couple of months—"

"I'm sorry Mr. Jonathan, but he'd like you to join him now."

Jonathan blinked. "Now? As in, *right now*, in Tokyo?"

"Yes. As soon as you pack your bags, we'll fly out. The pilot and plane are waiting on the tarmac at Sardy Field. Mr. Akira requested that you come immediately."

This was bizarre. He and Akira spoke every month for a few hours, and each knew how full the other's life was. "Is everything okay?"

The serious man shifted; a bit uncomfortable. "He was very firm. and I've been made aware you know how he can be when he asks firmly."

Jonathan couldn't help but smile, remembering Akira's ability to blend loving grace with intimidating intensity. "Yes, I definitely do." He turned and looked at Nakoma, who had a mischievous smile on her face. "Well, what do you say? Want to go to Japan?"

She'd met Akira a few times, and they had a deep and profound connection. She loved him from the beginning. Grandparents, or those that act like them, are the best, and she knew more than anyone how important Akira was in her dad's life. She didn't always love Akira's "chop wood carry water" dogma, but she deeply loved the man whose life inspired it.

Plus, a break from her world and the intense scrutiny she was under would be a breath of fresh air. "Yes! Let's go!"

* * *

An hour later, they watched Colorado grow smaller beneath the wings of the plane as they broke through the clouds.

With a 16-hour flight and the unknown ahead of them, Jonathan dove into work. As soon as he connected to the plane's Wi-Fi, he was bombarded with messages and emails. Running his company was normally plenty of work, but it was especially busy right now. They had an acquisition offer on the table, and that meant a lot more calls, emails, and messages than usual, on top of the extra paperwork to get through.

As Jonathan worked, Nakoma watched the clouds fly by. It felt liberating to be leaving the incident — and all of its complications — behind for a while. Staring out at the endless sky on the other side of the window, she turned her music up. Whatever waited for them in Japan, she was excited to be on the journey and to see the small man who always seemed to make her feel invincible.

CHAPTER 3

Tokyo

Jonathan and Nakoma stared at Tokyo's Imperial Palace, in awe of its grand architecture. Pink cherry blossoms fell from the trees, making the entire scene appear as magical as a fairytale. Then they heard a familiar voice behind them...

"Welcome to Tokyo!" They turned to find Akira walking toward them with the biggest smile.

Jonathan bowed, "Akira-sensei!" Jonathan was always shocked at how physically small Akira was in real life. The longer he was away from him, the larger he would grow in his mind. It happens that way sometimes with powerful figures in our lives.

Akira threw his arms around Jonathan in a warm hug. "It's good to see you, my friend. And you too, young lady! My little princess has grown up!!" He gave Nakoma a big hug. "Are you ready to see Tokyo with me?"

"Of course," Jonathan answered. "But I have to ask, is everything okay? It isn't often that we get flown around the world at the drop of a hat for nothing!"

"Everything will be fine, trust me. Thank you for coming. Let's just enjoy the time we have together!"

Jonathan didn't love his cryptic response, but he had learned the hard way, over and over again, that with Akira it was better to just trust him. He hated even more when he would reflexively tell him, "*You were right.*" The fire would burn deep in Akira's eyes, and then he would look into what felt like the bottom of your soul and say, "Nothing is more offensive, because I only speak when I believe in the deepest part of my being that what I am sharing is *Truth*. I don't need to be told I was right. I knew when I spoke that I was right…. or I wouldn't have wasted my breath."

For the rest of the day, Akira played tour guide, showing Jonathan and Nakoma around the city. They walked through Tokyo's parks, ate local foods, and enjoyed the city's iconic neighborhoods, from the bustling crowds of Ginza to the funky shops of Harajuku. Nakoma took it all in, amazed at the opportunity to see this beautiful city. Her competition and training schedule were so intense that they didn't get to travel for fun very often.

Near the end of the day, Akira told them, "I have a dinner event tonight, and I was hoping you two would join me. Jonathan nodded, as he could only imagine what his old mentor was up to: "We would love to."

* * *

Jonathan and Nakoma felt a little out of place as they were ushered into the massive ballroom at the Four Seasons hotel in the center of the city. It was a black-tie affair, and they whispered to each other that they felt underdressed!

Akira guided them to their seats in the VIP section, where they watched the event begin. One after another, awards were given out to important businessmen, civic leaders, and athletes. Jonathan felt a bit confused. What were they doing here?

Just when he was about to ask Akira, the final presentation of the night was announced: *The Order of the Rising Sun*, one of Japan's highest honors. As the name of its recipient was announced, Jonathan and Nakoma were stunned as the little man beside them rose to his feet: it was Akira.

He bowed politely to thunderous applause, before taking the stage. As he accepted the award, he addressed the gathering: "You know, at this point in my life, as much as I am incredibly honored by this, I truly don't need awards. I'm so blessed to look around this room and call many of you friends, and the experiences we have shared together mean more than any award ever could."

Akira continued: "But since I'm here, I'll share a few things I wish I had known when I was younger. One of the most beneficial things in the world, is to live life from a death lens perspective. So many people futilely and foolishly live as if they will never die. Strangely and ironically one of the freest and most powerful groups are those that have had to stare death in the face.

I realized how fragile life is and that I needed to live from a death bed perspective at a very young age. I was only a little boy when my baby brother drowned, and I was the one who found him and pulled him out of the pool.

While this perspective was tragically forced upon me, most people discover this reality later in life. Eventually though, we all are forced to face the inevitability of our mortality, and the wise choose to live from that lens instead of waiting until it springs upon them like a thief in the night.

I always found it funny when doctors say 'terminal' cancer, because we all are terminal. The only guarantee in life is death, yet so many live in a make-believe world where there are only happily ever after's.

We focus on all the wrong things. We allow shame, status, and ego to drive our lives. We ferociously climb the ladder, foolishly believing somewhere at the top is a pot of gold. But it's fool's gold and eventually we realize our ladder was on the wrong building the whole time. The only way to avoid this, is to live our lives from a death bed perspective.

So, I want to ask everyone in the room to reach under your seats, where you'll find a pen and a small notepad. What I want you to do, is answer the following question: *What do you want to be remembered for when you are gone from this earth?*

I call this the obituary exercise. Take a few minutes and truthfully answer that question. You can throw it away at the end if you'd like, don't worry. No one else has to see it and I'm not going to put anyone on the spot."

For a moment, the room was silent. Then, all you could hear were the sound of pens scratching across paper as everyone began doing the exercise.

Jonathan and Nakoma couldn't help but smile. Of course Akira would take the chance to transform what was supposed to be a public honor for himself into an awkward moment of making people do some ridiculously difficult, but incredibly important internal work. *He never missed a moment.* One of his greatest skills was not allowing awkwardness to keep him from doing what he knew in his gut he needed to do.

Sure enough, when Akira finished, he received a resounding standing ovation.

CHAPTER 4

One Final Mission

Afterward, Jonathan and Nakoma joined Akira in another black SUV, which drove them an hour away back to his home near Yokohoma, one of the lower-class areas outside of Tokyo. He ushered them inside, revealing a warm, quaintly decorated Japanese home. As he showed them to the guest room, Akira thanked them. "This was such a special day, and I'm so grateful you were both there."

"No problem," Jonathan couldn't help an edge of annoyance in his jet-lagged voice. "But I'm not sure that was worth flying us all the way around the world for."

"Say what you mean Jonathan, I've always appreciated that you don't mince words."

"It was great to see you get an award, but you know we have a lot going on in our lives right now. Nakoma has the X Games in 8 weeks. My business has a major deal on the table, but you flew us here to watch you give a speech? We know you couldn't care less about awards."

Akira shook his head in frustration, "Sometimes I wonder if I even trained you, and why you are my favorite student." He sighed, "Come with me."

He led them down the hall, opening a door to another room. They walked down into some sort of dingy basement. As the lights slowly flickered on, Jonathan and Nakoma couldn't help but gasp in surprise. It was obvious this place didn't have many visitors, at least not in many years. The room was full of awards, trophies and keepsakes. They covered the shelves and walls, each celebrating Akira. They were clearly collected from many different decades, indicating an entire lifetime filled with achievements — everything from martial arts tournaments to civic and social impact awards.

"Whoa..." Nakoma couldn't believe her eyes. "Is that you with the President?" She pointed to a framed photo on the wall.

"Which one? I've trained many Presidents from different parts of the world." Sure enough, there was Akira with many world leaders and dignitaries. Nakoma was stunned. Looking around, she realized how many of the photos showed him with athletes, celebrities, and leaders that even she recognized.

Even Jonathan was blown away, "Wait, is that you smoking a cigar with—"

"Yes," Akira interjected. "Yes, it is. Of all people, I thought you would at least be able to keep your jaw closed while looking at these photos."

"We talk a lot, but you never mentioned any of these people!"

Akira looked at him sternly, "I didn't need to. Only insecure people need to let you know who their friends and clients are."

He turned to Nakoma and softened, "I've been blessed to influence many people during my life. You and your father are two of the most important to me. That is why it is *you* that are here.

Trophies, awards, and deals are worthless from a death bed perspective, fleeting trinkets compared to what truly matters in life: *who we become and the impact we have on others.*

As much as I'm proud of what I've achieved in my life, my true wealth lies in the people I know and love. Trust me, you're here for a reason. One that's much more important than any award."

Jonathan, I have never asked you for anything, and I'm not going to start now. If I haven't earned your trust, then you are more foolish than you were when you arrived in Japan as an eighteen-year-old.

I have one final mission for you.

I would like you both to travel with me for the next month or so. It pains me to say this, but I trust no one else with this mission other than you Jonathan, and I won't tell you exactly what it is right now, but you are uniquely qualified and capable of completing it.

Even if you don't know exactly why you're here, just know that what we see, the memories we make, and the lessons we learn together, will change both of your lives. I can promise you that."

Jonathan nodded; a bit ashamed at his previous outburst. He processed what Akira was asking, realizing how costly it was. The timing was bad for him and Nakoma and the stress in his life was incredibly high. But Akira's words back at the hotel echoed in his mind...

*"On your death bed, will you look back on your life and see a life worthy of the gift you'd been given? Will you truthfully be able to look back at it all and say: 'I have run my race faithfully, leaving it all on the field... I have finished empty in the areas **that truly matter**.?"*

There was only one right answer: "Of course. It would be a privilege and an honor to do one last mission for you sensei."

Jonathan turned to Nakoma, "You've been training so hard for the X Games. Even though we can still do training without being on the mountain, taking more than a month off will be a big disruption. Are you okay with that?"

"Dad, didn't he teach you that *everything is training?* We both know that most of what makes me special on the mountain happens far away from it." For the first time since the incident, Nakoma had that unmistakable twinkle back in her eyes, and an excitement in her voice. Even though she hadn't spent a ton of time with Akira, she treasured the time they'd been given and was excited for more of it. She had her mother's intuition, and when she trusted it, it was undefeated.

Tears sprang up in Akira's eyes, as he beamed with joy. He had influenced tens of millions of people on the planet, but there were certain people who mattered most to him, and Nakoma had always been near the top of that list.

CHAPTER 5

The *S.S.E.* Beast

The next morning, Jonathan woke up early. Shaking off his jet lag, he walked into Akira's office with a triple espresso in hand. His office was very different than the basement full of awards and pictures. The office was minimalistic and beautiful, like something Steve Jobs designed.

He looked up to his mentor more than anyone, and he knew Akira was incredibly wise. Still, even after living around him for a decade and knowing he was one of his closest friends, he had no idea that the old man was so well connected and regarded among so many powerful people. At the same time, he wasn't entirely shocked: it made sense that the wisdom Akira embodied could impact the world — Jonathan had seen that personally, as it was the backbone of Jonathan's most famous book.

There it was: the only thing that stood out in the office, almost out of place. Under Akira's famous samurai bow and a quiver of arrows was a beautiful shadow box with Jonathan's book, and the handwritten note Jonathan had given Akira many years ago…

Chop Wood, Carry Water. The global sensation and international viral best seller that people from all walks of life swore by as their favorite and most important book.

Akira never made a big deal of it when Jonathan talked to him about it. The story of his apprenticeship under Akira as a samurai archer sold slowly at first, but similar to Jonathan's growth and maturation under Akira it continued to grow into a behemoth. Every week Jonathan would see someone mention the impact it had in their life on TV or in some article or podcast. Even now, the book's reach and impact took Jonathan by surprise. All he had done was put down what he had learned as honestly as possible, and — just as Akira had taught him — *surrender the outcome, trust the process.*

"How does that make you feel, seeing your book as the crown jewel in my office?" Akira had silently entered the room, looking up at the book.

"Incredibly proud," Jonathan beamed.

It was clear Akira was proud too. But he also seemed troubled. "I'm glad our story has inspired people — but our relationship is a lot more important. After all, this is just a book. Is the commercial success of that book going to matter on your deathbed? Our relationship is much more important than that to me. That book has done incredible things in the world, but it has also been co-opted by transactional leaders who use it as a cudgel to drive results from their teams, instead of using it from a heart posture of love, to serve, equip, empower, and inspire them.

It seems the wisdom and truth of "trust the process" has been transformed into trite bulletin board-, bumper sticker-, and T shirt-material for transactional leaders who really only care about the next win, the next title, and their next higher profile position.

The true message was lost and instead became fuel for selfish ulterior motives.

These people prioritize trophies over hearts, position over purpose, the outcome over the process, money over everything, and in so doing, damage the people entrusted to their leadership. They have taken what you meant to be a transformation of being, and they use it instead as a manipulative tool to try and achieve poriferous goals.

In fact, I was recently sent a clip of a famous college baseball coach who referenced *Chop Wood Carry Water* as a touchstone for how he ran his team. Then, in the same breath, he lamented that he had '764 innings' walking out the door at the end of the season.

The man literally couldn't even refer to his players as human beings. Instead, he talked about them like productivity units. He talked about the book as if it were a productivity manual. How often did we get deep into the nitty gritty of productivity during our time together?"

Jonathan actually laughed out loud at the thought. "Not once in over ten years!"

"Exactly!" Akira exclaimed with a rare edge of frustration. "It made me question whether or not this guy actually read a word of your book!"

Akira continued shaking his head in disgust, "Sadly, so many 'successful' people are operating from what I call the SSE model."

"SSE?" Jonathan's eyebrows rose.

"Shame, Status, and Ego. It's a trap that many are drawn into in life. They may 'win' in the short game, but they lose the long game. Shame is the enemy's greatest weapon.

When you empty yourself of ego and fear, you can be filled up with love, peace, contentment, joy, and courage. This is one of the greatest challenges because so many people leading others operate out of their ego and not their heart. Nevertheless, we must empty our ego daily so we can fulfill our potential rather than simply placating our lowest self.

Ego is a ravenous beast that poisons everything it encounters, no matter the achievements.
Ego might get things done, but it will ruin a lot of what really matters along the way.

We don't have time today, but I want to tell you about the difference between Ego dreams and Soul dreams."

"And I want to hear it," Jonathan replied. "Right now, I need to wake Nakoma up. I have some calls to get through this morning, but I can join you later. I also have to look up 'poriferous'."

Akira chuckled. "Don't worry about Nakoma. I'll take her into Shibuya and the cool shops. With you as her father, she could obviously use my help with fashion."

Jonathan laughed, and couldn't disagree. Akira did have impeccable fashion, something that he'd never been able to pass on to Jonathan no matter how hard he tried.

CHAPTER 6

Freedom of Choice

Shibuya, Tokyo.

With a buzz, the light shifted from red to green, and within seconds Shibuya Crossing was flooded with people. Hundreds of pedestrians walked across one of the busiest intersections in the world, while Akira and Nakoma watched from a nearby tea shop.

As Akira sipped his tea, Nakoma nodded to the passing crowds…"I can't believe no one's bumping into each other!" Sure enough, the pedestrians moved around one another with silent, clockwork precision.

Akira nodded. "Fitting in and not rocking the boat have always been one of this country's greatest strengths, but also one of its greatest downfalls."

"What do you mean?"

"I've always loved my homeland, but as I grew up, it began to bother me to live in a culture that so prioritized buying into the system over individual freedom. That's one reason I chose to live all over the world as an adult, and not just here in Japan. I learned how big the world is and became liberated from the dogma of my people. There is a saying here, *'the nail that stands out gets hammered down.'* I wanted more for my life."

Nakoma nodded, but then indicated a passing group of teenaged girls, all dressed in wildly colorful and creative clothing. "Seems like there's more individual freedom nowadays."

"There is," agreed Akira. "Yet the progress has been slow and painful. Suicide and rampant abuse of alcohol are nationwide issues, driven in many cases by demanding cultural and family expectations that force millions of people to trade their lives for social and familial acceptance instead of passion, purpose, and fulfillment.

And while no one understands the value of relentlessly chasing excellence more than me, I also know this — if the path to mastery isn't personally meaningful, it can become the exact opposite: empty and soul-crushing. That's one reason it's been so difficult to watch your father's book be so misused in cultures where people are more prized for their output instead of their inherent worth.

In the more individualistic cultures of the West, *Chop Wood Carry Water* and the "trust the process" system it lays out, has set countless people free to follow their own journeys toward greatness. But in cultures or subcultures that prize systems and results over hearts and human beings, that book has been used as another empty tool to drive the mandates of a "leader."

While that book is many things, a plug-and-play 'how to' guide to performance is absolutely not one of them!"

Nakoma grinned at the older man's burst of passion. And as the light changed, she looked over the waiting crowd of pedestrians again. A sea of dark business suits, white shirts, neatly tied ties, and briefcases. Everyone looked the same, like God had taken the 'copy + paste' function and used it on human beings.

She couldn't help but wonder, "Why is it so hard for people to live authentically and different from those around them?"

"The short answer," Akira replied, "Is that not everyone had parents like yours!"

She laughed, as he continued, "The long answer has to do with freedom. The hard truth is that total freedom—the ability to be or become whoever you like, to do or go wherever you want — is so terrifying that most people absolutely refuse it when given the chance to have it. They run the other direction as fast as they can."

"Really?" Nakoma hesitated. "Why would someone do that?"

"Because true freedom removes your excuses and creates total responsibility. If you're free, <u>YOU</u> possess the power to take action over your situation, which means <u>YOU</u> are accountable for your actions. That kind of responsibility is a beast that most will avoid at all costs.

People are so terrified by real responsibility, that they will gladly accept the roles, excuses, and problems handed to them by their environment to avoid it — all while insisting they can't do anything about it. Sometimes they will even choose a life in prison over a life with real responsibility — a prison constructed by their excuses about what's keeping them from the life of their dreams:

'The government'
'My parents'
'My coach'
'My wife'
'My husband'
'My girlfriend/boyfriend'
'My genes'

'My neighborhood'
'My teachers'

The world is overflowing with legitimate excuses, yet excuses do nothing to make our life better. They only make us feel better, and that it is not our fault.

The truth is that others do impact us, but ultimately; *we are the ones with the controller in our hands.*

Most people are more comfortable acquiescing to the system or their environment than facing the discomfort and pain required to break off and take responsibility for what they have control over.

The reality is that if you only follow the rules, fit in, and do what you're told, one day you will wake up and wonder what happened to your life. The mask you put on to survive and fit in has now become a permanent part of your identity.

No amount of drugs, alcohol, video games, money, women, men, power, vacations, watches, cars, or homes, can overcome or fill the need to live the life and do the things we know in our soul we were meant to do.

Nelson Mandela spent 27 years in prison. Do you think he would have traded his life or impact for any of those things? We know the answer, he wasn't even willing to trade it for his freedom. They offered it many times, and he chose to stay in prison until his mission outside was accomplished.

Mother Teresa spent her time with people suffering from leprosy. Do you think she would have traded her life for riches?

Malala got shot in the face for standing up to the Taliban and fighting for women's rights and access to education. Do you think she would trade her life for those superficial things?

These people are human, not superheroes. They had seasons where they wanted to quit, where they were depressed, and questioned whether taking the road less traveled and being uniquely who they were made to be was actually worth it.

Ultimately, what you come to realize when you choose to really live is that the challenges, the fear, the adversity, the storms, the trials, the injustice, the betrayals, are all a torturous yet essential and unavoidable part of the mosaic of a *truly successful* life."

Nakoma nodded, in awe of the little man. "How did you learn all of this?"

Akira shrugged, "Thankfully, I had people come into my life that trained me well from the time I was your age. Like you, I experienced great loss early in my life, but hard things are a blessing long term if you let them be."

Nakoma was quiet, but knew he was right. She didn't often talk about losing her mother, and neither did Jonathan. Her unexpected death five years ago was the hardest time in either of their lives. She didn't like talking about it, but she also knew that Akira understood. The first time she met him was at her mother's funeral. From the moment she met him it was as if their hearts were somehow synced; he intuitively understood things about her no one else did, not even Jonathan. They were kindred souls and 'spirit animals' as they called each other sometimes.

She was grateful to be around him again.

"The harsh truth is that if you do not have the courage and conviction to be uniquely who you were created to be, you will look back on your life with profound regret at the life you should have lived."

Nakoma nodded, "All because excuses are easier than responsibility."

"Exactly! Accepting that you have freedom of choice — to leave a bad job, move cities, move countries, break off a toxic relationship, or improve yourself in any way — requires accepting that you are personally accountable for what you do with that freedom. There are *prosequences* and *consequences* to our choices. We do not all start in the same place, but where we start does not determine who we become and where we finish. It impacts it for sure, but it is not *THE* determining factor. *WE* are.

Most people are so allergic to personal accountability they would rather lie to themselves — and the world — and claim they don't have a choice.

The reality, of course, is that you *always* have a choice, no matter your circumstances. Even if you're living in a concentration camp facing death every day, you still have a choice. Just ask Victor Frankl — his book *Man's Search For Meaning* describes the choices that he made in the prison camp at Auschwitz, and it has become one of the most beloved and inspirational books ever written.

But enough of that for now!" Akira finished his last sip of tea. "I forgot to ask: did you bring a good outdoor jacket?"

"I think so," she replied. "Why?"

"Because you'll need one where we're going next. Let's go find you a really cool one!"

Nakoma smiled and perked up. Her dad didn't love shopping, and she missed shopping with her mom. Akira was very attuned to this, and it was one of the first things they did when they were together.

They went to some really cool stores, and then to get a mani-pedi. She loved her dad, but "he would never."

CHAPTER 7

The Most Joyful Place on Earth

Paro, Bhutan.

"It is sad Akira's fashion sense hasn't rubbed off on you, Dad." Nakoma quipped while looking at the group photo she had just snapped. "We need you to step your game up!" They all chuckled, and with the way Jonathan was dressed compared to the other two, even he had to agree. Ever since his wife had passed, shopping for clothes wasn't something he enjoyed.

"Mind if I go ahead?" Nakoma was tired of going at their slower pace.

"Of course! We'll be right behind you."

Nakoma took off, following the trail further up the mountain. She was breathing hard from the thin air, and even felt some sweat despite the chilly weather. But she forgot about all of it when she reached the summit. At the top of the trail was a beautiful monastery, overlooking the most breathtaking view she'd ever seen. Under a bright blue sky, massive snow-capped peaks spread across the horizon, and she could see the village they started at far down below in the valley.

Nakoma squinted. Beneath the shelter of the monastery, she saw hundreds of tiny pyramidal sculptures. Some were painted gold, others were painted red, but mostly they were either white or a natural earth tone.

A few minutes later, Jonathan and Akira reached the monastery as well. As Akira caught his breath, he looked out over the view and smiled. "Beautiful, isn't it?"

Jonathan nodded. "Something tells me we aren't here for the beauty."

Akira smiled. "You didn't think Nakoma and I brought you here so we could show off our new outfits?!"

As Jonathan shook his head, Akira went on. "Okay, you're right. I was brought here when I was very young, to learn valuable lessons about life and death. Do you see those tiny pyramids everywhere?"

Nakoma nodded, "I wondered what they were."

"Those are *tsa tsa's*, memorials to those who've passed on. They're molded by monks from the leftover ashes of cremation pyres. They are commissioned in remembrance by family members: for the people of Bhutan, daily life is interwoven very closely with death.

In fact, they are expected to pause and meditate on death three times a day.

In many cultures, especially in the West, death is kept out of sight, or hidden entirely. The sick and elderly are kept in nursing homes or hospitals, and before they're buried, the dead are made to look as 'lifelike' as possible. Even meat is raised and butchered at farms far away from those who eat it, instead of being raised or hunted by hand.

Many people do their best not to think at all about death, erroneously believing that doing so will make their lives darker or more depressing. But the complete opposite is true. *Living your life in the light of your inevitable death actually releases you to live more fully.* It is a similar paradox to surrendering the outcome, where surrendering actually allows your skill to shine through. In the same way, facing death allows you to be more fully alive.

This beautiful country is one of the poorest economically in the world. But guess what? It's also one of the most joyful places on earth, consistently ranking as happier than most wealthier countries on the global index.

92% of Bhutanese describe themselves as happy!

As a child I thought it was incredibly weird that they focused on death. Now I know it is incredibly wise. After all, it is only through the light of death that we can see what is most valuable in life. That is why so many people who overcome cancer live more fulfilled lives than before they were diagnosed.

The only guarantees in life are pain and death. We are not guaranteed joy, peace, health, or wealth. The one thing I can tell you with absolute certainty about your life, is that you won't get out of it alive. We all have expiration dates.

You have now, maybe today, and possibly tomorrow. That goes on until, one day, it doesn't. One day, your days and moments are gone in an instant.

If we aren't promised tomorrow or next year, the question becomes: what should we do with the time we have?"

Nakoma paused, realizing that Akira was looking right at her. She shifted uncomfortably, looking to Jonathan. But he nodded at her. Jonathan had always made it clear that he would provide her with incredible opportunities, but he would never prepare the road for her. He would always support, but never enable. He would only prepare her for the possibilities of what may lie ahead on the road.

She thought about it for a long moment. "You should treat today and people as you would if it was your last opportunity with them?"

Akira's wrinkled face broke into a huge smile. "Your daughter is very wise, Jonathan."

He nodded with pride, "Definitely wiser than I was at that age!"

Akira went on, "Too many people wait until it's too late. They live a life that ends up packed with regrets. They get caught up in the addiction to busyness. They get caught up chasing outcomes instead of falling in love with the process. They get stuck chasing things instead of experiences. They get focused on achievements instead of remembering that relationships are really what truly matter.

The impact we have on others, and who we become in the process, that's really it. The other stuff is cool, but it cannot fill the void we are trying to fill. In fact, sometimes achieving and getting that stuff only makes the chasm greater.

If we take care of the foundational things, the rest falls into place as it should. When we don't, at best we end up with fool's gold, and at worst we sacrifice what truly matters at the altar of *potentially* winning."

CHAPTER 8

A Single Player Game

Akira and Nakoma sipped green tea, watching the throngs of people in front of them. While Jonathan worked back at the hotel, they were taking a break from exploring the city and doing a little bit of local shopping. In front of them, hundreds of people moved from store to store or clustered around tables, sharing food or having conversations.

Akira watched them with interest, then looked at Nakoma. "Nakoma, a great irony of life is that you must find balance between two truths that seem to be the opposite of one another.

The first is that the key to a beautiful life is relationships. The world's longest study of human development was conducted by Harvard. Beginning in 1938, the researchers took down data on the lives of two groups of men. No matter their economic advantages or cultural privilege when the study began, the only thing that mattered when it came to them living a long and fulfilling life was simple — the quality of their relationships.

The better their relationships, the longer, healthier, and happier their lives. The men with great relationships were healthier, less prone to addiction, and rebounded from unexpected difficulties and tragedies much faster than their lonelier counterparts. On the other hand, the men who were unsatisfied in their relationships lived shorter, sicker lives, no matter how wealthy or privileged they were in their earlier years.

So, if you want to live a long, healthy, fulfilling life, even the data says that the active ingredient is your relationship to others.

Yet, on the other hand, living your life according to the wishes and expectations of others is a recipe for ending up becoming trapped in a life you hate.

In Bonnie Ware's book, *The Top Five Regrets Of The Dying*, the number one regret was, 'I wish I had the courage to live the life I knew I was supposed to live instead of living according to everyone else's expectations.'

Yes, our relationship to others is a central ingredient in a life well-lived. But our lives are our own, and only we are responsible for how we live them.

Yes, others' actions affect how we are raised, and create wounds we receive as we go through life. Eventually though, the higher your consciousness becomes, the more you realize that life is all about choices and maximizing or squandering whatever potential you have.

Throughout life there will be no shortage of well-intentioned advice from well-meaning people around you. Some of that advice will be life-giving, and some of it will be absolutely terrible. Unfortunately, even those who love us most will at times mistakenly give us advice that isn't in our best interest. Their advice may in fact be best for them and is in the interest of keeping the status quo. When this happens, it is our job to recognize it and act accordingly, even if we risk disappointing those who love and care for us.

After nearly eighty years on this planet, I still haven't found a way to live a life worth living that doesn't risk disappointing those who love me the most.

In fact, here's what I've learned instead: our job, throughout life, is to disappoint as many people as it takes to avoid disappointing ourselves on our death bed.

Why? The truth is that life is a single player game and the controller is in your hand.

When you come into this world, it doesn't feel that way. As a toddler you only have access to two buttons, A and B. Crying or smiling.

Which is why a toddler responds the way they do to situations that overwhelm them. They can only use 'A, B', 'A, B' — the most basic responses possible.

The sad thing is, many adults who've never gained awareness or emotional maturity hold on to that same controller from back when they were a child. Have you ever seen an adult throw a hissy fit, a real temper tantrum just like a toddler? That's because they haven't upgraded the software in the controller of their brain. When they're confronted with a situation that overwhelms them, they lack the buttons on their controller to react with patience, intentionality, nuance and wisdom.

Now, the opposite can be true as well. Even someone your age can have a much more advanced controller for their age. As you gain awareness and skills, you add entire new rows of buttons. The ability to remain calm in conflict, to persist through difficulty, and to navigate complex problems without allowing your emotions to overwhelm you — all of those require a more advanced software upgrade."

Nakoma nodded, "Ya, sometimes I feel like an alien with kids my age, because even though my dad can be a lot for me sometimes, he has helped me develop a very advanced controller."

Akira smiled, "Ya, I'm sorry about that." As they both chuckled, he continued, "But I agree. Your father has given you different buttons than most:

-beneficial and constructive self-talk
-retraining the signal
-adjusting your warrior dial
-being fully present
-fuel for your heart
-heart posture of gratitude
-growth mindset
-surrendering the outcome
-willingness to endure

With these buttons, along with the others that you have been working to develop from a very young age, you have a very different type of controller in your hand than most.

Sadly, humans love to upgrade their phones, cars, homes, and clothes — but it is incredibly rare to see them actively trying to upgrade the software in their brain that is the only control they have over their life.

A lot of things in life happen outside of our control, but how we play the game all depends on the controller in our hands."

CHAPTER 9

Soul Dreams vs. Ego Dreams

The airplane cabin was quiet. Nakoma slept soundly in her seat as Jonathan rubbed his eyes. He'd been working almost nonstop since they took off, and he was exhausted. But there was still plenty to do. As the head of a company that bore his name, he knew it was up to him to ensure that the deal got across the finish line.

"Long workday?" Akira stirred from where he sat across from Jonathan and shut the book he'd been reading. He could see how exhausted Jonathan was.

"Yes. Also, difficult and frustrating. I'd even say crazy! But, like you taught me, the grind never stops."

"Hmm. I'm not sure about that, actually."

"What?! That's what you taught me!"

"I taught you to put first things first. Is what you're working on truly a 'first thing'? When you arrive at your death bed, will you look back on it with gratitude for the wisdom you showed by pursuing it? Because the words you just used to describe it were 'difficult' 'frustrating' and 'crazy'. Do those sound like words you'd use to describe first things?"

Jonathan shook his head. "I guess not."

"Tell me about what has you so frustrated and crazed. What are you dealing with?" The old man's gaze seemed to cut right through him.

Jonathan knew better than to hide anything. He filled Akira in on his situation — a private equity firm, one of the biggest in the world, was interested in acquiring his business. A crucial part of that acquisition had to do with retaining Jonathan's name on the business. After all, his reputation and personal brand as an athlete had been a critical ingredient in building his business in the first place.

The deal seemed straightforward. Jonathan would get a huge pay day, all without having to work too much more than he already was, and in a few years, he would transition out of the business completely. It was the culmination of a decade of hard work.

Still, Akira didn't seem enthused. He simply asked, "Remember what Francis Chan said, 'Our greatest fear should not be of failure, but of succeeding at things that don't really matter'?" Jonathan nodded. "Well, did you dream of getting acquired by a huge PE firm when you were a kid?"

That thought stuck with Jonathan for a long moment. Around them, the airplane cabin was silent. Finally, he had to admit the truth: "No. I didn't."

Akira nodded. "I didn't think so. Would it be cool? Sure. But is that being relentless in the pursuit of what sets your soul on fire? Because *that*, is what I taught you. *I want, wanted, and will always want you to be relentless in the pursuit of what sets your soul on fire.*

To me, it looks like you are caught up in chasing an ego dream. A dream that society thinks is valuable. A dream that other people will tell you is important. But will it matter on your death bed? I doubt it.

I won't tell you what to do. I'll only remind you of this: don't get caught up chasing ego dreams, and end up sacrificing your health, your peace, and your most important relationships in the process."

Jonathan nodded. For the thousandth time, Akira had given him a lot to think about.

CHAPTER 10

Lessons in Time

Melbourne, Australia.

"Who are we here to meet, again?"

Carrying their bags, Jonathan and Nakoma followed Akira through a huge airplane hangar, passing several gleaming private jets. Despite the fact that he claimed they had a schedule to keep, he didn't explain what exactly that schedule contained — he only told them when they needed to be at the airport next.

"Dave is a very good friend of mine. He's the one helping us with all the air travel. And, he just so happened to be the head of global sales for one the world's biggest airlines."

"Okay, that makes a lot more sense!" Jonathan laughed.

I shouldn't be surprised, he thought, *Of course Akira has a friend who's been willing to help fly us all around the world like this*. Even though Jonathan had known the older man for more than two decades, Akira still surprised him sometimes.

Today was no different. As Akira led them down the line of private jets, a little man with crazy curly hair shooting up everywhere exited the last one.

Akira greeted him joyfully, "Dave Hilfman!"

The moment he spotted Akira, Dave broke into a broad grin. "Sensei!!" His voice boomed as he wrapped Akira in a tight hug, "and you must be the legends Jonathan and Nakoma. I've heard so much about you!"

Jonathan liked him immediately. His wide smile and contagious energy were infectious, and he had a fun-loving gleam in his eye that instantly reminded Jonathan of Akira. He seemed to know about the 'mission' that Akira had spoken to them about — though his smile faltered a little bit when he mentioned it, something that Jonathan noted but couldn't quite figure out.

"Well, how's it going so far? I know you've only made it to a few of your stops."

"So far it's been beautiful," Akira smiled. "We currently need to get to Paris. Think you could help with that?"

"Funny you should ask," Dave nodded to the plane behind him: "Four of my team had to pivot and fly home to our hub, but I still need to get to London by tomorrow, so I've got a few extra seats. Would love for you to join me, and we can drop you in Paris no problem!"

Nakoma and Jonathan just laughed. At this point, they'd come to expect the unexpected with Akira.

* * *

A few hours later, they were crossing the ocean and enjoying the plane's roomy seats. Akira caught Dave up on their travels, noting the destinations they'd already visited.

"Sounds like you're making good time so far," Dave noted.

Akira chuckled, "I don't know that we're 'making' any more time than we've already been given. But we're certainly trying to take full advantage of the time that we do have."

Dave nodded, "That's the tricky part, isn't it? You can't beat time. But I've learned that you can slow it, stretch it, and — with enough wisdom — learn to spend it in ways that can even seem to stop it, at least for a little while."

Nakoma chimed in, puzzled, "How did you learn that, and can you teach me?"

"Well, the short answer is that I learned it the hard way. The longer answer is that I lost my wife unexpectedly many years ago. I've been told you've experienced a similar loss, so I know you're aware that in the midst of all the pain, there's wisdom to be found.

In my case, that loss became my teacher. The first class it taught me was about time.

As an executive of a global conglomerate, I always thought of my time in terms of quarterly goals, yearly reports, and daily or weekly schedules. I planned things months, years in advance. I had so many long-term plans — when I would get promoted, when I would have a certain number in my bank account, when I would retire.

But when my Tracey died, I learned in the most painful way possible, that tomorrow isn't guaranteed. We only get one life, and it can end at any time.

So, what happens when your life is cut short by a few decades? What happens when you have six months or two years to live?

What changes when you can no longer make a 20-year plan or even a six-month plan?

It brings all of your 'tomorrow I'll do this' and 'next year we can do that's a lot closer.

Those '*somedays*' become '*todays*' very quickly when you live life from a death bed perspective. The idea of, 'I'm going to do X after... ' goes out the window."

Remembering his own experience learning those hard truths, Jonathan added, "It certainly brings clarity around what matters and what does not. Like C.S. Lewis said, no one is more creative than when justifying their own behavior. The more successful you become, the easier it is to believe that you can control time — after all, you feel like you control so much else."

As the conversation continued, he couldn't help thinking of his own situation. Looking at his own life from a death bed perspective, would his company's acquisition truly matter in the end? He wasn't sure he liked the answer.

While Jonathan was lost in thought, Akira chimed in, "When you are struggling with what to do, a great exercise is to fast forward five years in your mind. Knowing everything you know about you, your strengths, weaknesses, triggers, unique story, and personal challenges, what advice would the more mature and wiser version of yourself give to you? Often, we look to others for advice as a way of letting ourselves off the hook, a built in excuse. Truth is, no one knows us like we know ourselves."

CHAPTER 11

Finding Your Sweet Spot

Paris, France.

Nakoma and Akira were enjoying a tasty meal at 'Philippe's,' which has been in business and beloved by the community for nearly a century, "this place has stayed in business while many others have failed because the people who run it know a very important truth...

Every little thing matters.

A restaurant that serves this many people each night at this high of a level is a delicately balanced team environment, where excellence depends on every detail. If the person who washes forks doesn't do their job, a diner's entire experience could be ruined."

"Really?" Nakoma squinted. "Because of a dirty fork?"

"Of course! If the guy who washes dishes thinks, 'I just do the dishes, I'm not that important... I can screw up and it won't matter. After all, it's just a fork,' and then they allow a dirty fork back out into the restaurant, it could ruin someone's experience and cost the restaurant greatly. In an environment like this, there are no small jobs. Even washing a fork matters greatly.

Sensei Yamashita taught me that if I wanted to be truly great, I needed to humble myself and understand that everyone and everything matters. Nothing like washing dishes to teach you that, and that was one of the first jobs he had me get.

One of my favorite quotes is "If a man is called to be a street sweeper, he should sweep streets even as Michaelangelo painted, or Beethoven composed music or Shakespeare wrote poetry. He should sweep streets so well that all the hosts of heaven and earth will pause to say, 'Here lived a great street sweeper who did his job well."

Nakoma smiled, "That is really powerful and thought provoking. Whose quote was that?"

"Dr. Martin Luther King Jr."

For a long moment, they were both silent. Nakoma had never thought of certain jobs that way, and it certainly made her think twice about what was happening in her own life. She never doubted that snowboarding was what she would do with her life, at least until the incident. Now, she wasn't quite as certain, because at times it no longer felt worth the intense life scrutiny she opened herself up to by living her life in the arena and the public eye.

Akira seemed to sense what she was thinking. "Is there anything you'd like to talk about?"

She shook her head. "Not right now."

Akira nodded, continuing, "Well, I know enough about what happened to tell you this: I have had the privilege of accomplishing amazing things in life, things most people never even dream of doing, and I have also made stupid, terrible decisions and experienced terrible failures. But neither my success nor my failures define me. As a society we are obsessed with reducing our fellow humans to one dimensional characters, but the truth is that humans have many, many dimensions. We are not defined by our best moments or choices, nor should we be defined solely by our worst moments or choices.... No matter what strangers on the internet say." He winked at her.

For a moment, they sat in silence. His words of wisdom and loving presence helped her put the incident in a better light, but she still didn't feel comfortable talking about it and changed the subject after pondering his words.

"So, what happened after washing dishes?" She asked. "How did you get to the point where you were training world leaders?"

"Great question! The long answer we don't have time for today. The short answer was when my sensei helped me answer the questions that revealed my sweet spot."

"Your what?" Nakoma said confused.

"My sweet spot! Here's how it works—" As he spoke, Akira drew a triangle on a napkin, labeling each point. "Finding your sweet spot involves answering these three questions:

1) What does the world need?
2) What am I great at?
3) What am I passionate about?"

When he finished, his drawing looked like this:

WHAT DOES THE WORLD NEED?

YOUR SWEET SPOT

WHAT ARE YOU
GREAT AT?

WHAT ARE YOU
PASSIONATE ABOUT?

When you are trying to figure out what you are supposed to be doing in life, just come back to this triangle and answer each question honestly. Then whatever overlaps each answer, that is where you need to be — regardless of how crazy people tell you you are. In fact, *especially* if everyone thinks you are crazy.

When I made the radical choice to live and serve in a homeless shelter, many people thought I was crazy. When I went into the slums and trained the athletes there, people thought I was crazy. When I was living with Okasan for many years as an adult, my peers thought I was crazy."

Nakoma nodded, realizing — the more she learned about Akira's life, the more she thought it made sense that people would think he was crazy. Ironically, this was one of her favorite things about him.

CHAPTER 12

It Takes What It Takes

Geneva, Switzerland.

"Have you ever had hot chocolate like this?" Jonathan asked Nakoma, while wiping a chocolate 'mustache' from his lip.

She shook her head, no. "If I had, I'd never forget it!"

They sat across from Akira, tucked into a booth inside a charming cafe. Akira smiled, "That's because the Swiss do it like no one else does."

"I'm sure we aren't here just for the hot chocolate. What are we really doing here? Jonathan inquired.

That special Akira twinkle entered his eyes. "We're here to go back to one of my favorite places. I'll give you a hint." He adjusted his shirt cuff, revealing a flash of his timepiece — a Platinum Presidential, one of his three favorite pieces.

It hit Jonathan suddenly. "Rolex! They make those here, right?"

Akira. "Yes. And we're going to visit the shop where I bought this, many years ago—"

"Akira?" A man's voice interjected. They turned to find a man with wild Einstein looking blonde hair approaching. He wore a comic tee shirt one size too small and a very mischievous smile. He vibrated with that distinctive kind of energy that meant he was either a drug addict that lived on the street, or some kind of a world class savant.

"I can't believe it's you, Akira!"

Akira wrapped him in a hug. Then he pulled away, introducing him to Jonathan and Nakoma. "This is my dear friend Ben. Ben is the best watch customizer in the world. He is the one who made the custom Daytona for me."

Ben chuckled, shaking Jonathan and Nakoma's hands. "He's too kind. What are you doing back here?"

"I should ask you the same thing!"

"I'm in the process of moving my operation to Dubai. So while I wait for my paperwork to go through, I've set up shop here."

"Excellent! We'll have to visit."

"Of course. But first, did I hear that you're heading to Rolex?" Akira nodded, and Ben smiled, "Don't worry, we can do better than just seeing the shop. Let me take care of it."

* * *

A few hours later, they were walking the factory line at Rolex. They passed the machining area, where technicians operated state-of-the-art CNC (Computer Numerical Control) machines with surgical precision, carving out the intricate components that form the heart of a Rolex watch.

As they passed by, Ben explained. "Don't let the machines fool you. While they do help with some of the tasks, every watch here is assembled and finished by human hands. That's one reason why each Rolex takes a year to make."

"A year?!" Nakoma was blown away. "For just a watch?"

"A Rolex isn't just a watch. It's wearable art, a timepiece that many of its wearers pass down to their children, and their children's children. It's not uncommon for a Rolex or Patek Philippe to be passed down for multiple generations, outliving multiple members of the family that at one time called it their own."

They entered the assembly area, where watchmakers used tools to fit together the movements, dials, and cases with clockwork precision. Every movement was precise, almost choreographed, but it was clear that reverence flourished at the heart of each worker's focus and attention.

"To simply make a watch, you can do that in a factory in a few hours. But to craft a timepiece that will last for centuries, and not only hold its value, but exponentially gain value, well that takes what it takes. Just like in everything, *greatness takes what it takes. There are no shortcuts, and no easy paths.*

Much like I spent a decade teaching your father on his journey to becoming a Samurai Archer, no matter what your craft, I hope that you always stamp your essence on it in a way that will outlive you.

Any time you feel like mailing it in, make sure you ask yourself those questions.

If you are making a product, ask yourself, am I making this with the attention to detail and durability that it can last for generations? And if your craft is more of a service, then ask, if I were under the brightest of lights and everyone in the world could see me, would I be proud of everything I have done and given that is under my control?"

CHAPTER 13

Persistence & Immediacy

Ignoring the bright lights and noise of the gymnastics facility around her, Nakoma took a deep breath before bursting into a sprint. With each stride, her focus narrowed, honing in on the vault ahead— she hit the springboard and launched off it, throwing her body into a twist as she shot into the air. She spun once — twice — and then — *wham!!* — her feet slammed into the mat, sticking the landing. She breathed heavily, satisfied.

"Well done!" Nearby, Akira nodded his approval. "That's eight in a row."

Nakoma nodded, taking a drink of water. "Last year my max was two."

"That's quite a difference. What changed?"

"I had to work on my landings. That meant changing my mobility routine and building strength in my right leg, which always used to slip. It made a big difference."

"I know you have a lot of great people on your team," Akira replied, "But that shows a tremendous amount of persistence, Nakoma. It's very rare for someone your age."

"What do you mean?"

"Persistence is a lost art. You see, your generation is incredibly unique, with so much potential. But you face an incredibly difficult task.

On one hand, you live in a world of absolute immediacy. You've grown up in a world where the bulk of the world's knowledge — powerful information which has, by and large, been closely and ferociously guarded by governments, authorities, and institutions for the majority of human history — is as easy to access as a single sentence typed into a search engine.

Remember that prior to the invention of the printing press about six hundred years ago, information was communicated by memory through the oral tradition, or by hand-printing every letter of it into books. That's an incredibly time-intensive and costly transmission system!

By comparison, information these days is incredibly cheap. No one has to remember it, and it doesn't cost much of anything to store or transmit it.

Information can be power, certainly. But in our world today, until you do something with it, it's useless. All of the information in the world cannot guarantee mastery. Just look around you: has the Information Age magically turned anyone with access to information into a master of their craft? Has it suddenly produced more geniuses or brilliant artists or inventors than the Renaissance?

Of course it hasn't! If anything, it has produced fewer. And that's because of a simple truth: information might cost less than ever, but the cost of greatness remains the same.

So while your generation lives in a world of immediacy where every piece of information it would take to become great is available right now, for free, they also live in a world where greatness will remain inevitably out of reach to 99.99%, because they have been conditioned that things should come as fast and easy as the technology around them.

Greatness and mastery will always require incredible patience, deliberate practice, failure, and an insane willingness to endure. All of these qualities are challenging to develop, much more so in a world where speed and immediacy surround you.

If you don't have the grit to get past all the no's and continually fail forward in spite of the shame and heartbreak, you won't make it to greatness.

Greatness asks these questions of us every day:

"How much are you willing to suffer?"
"How long will you keep showing up?"
"How many days of Hell Week can you take and not ring the bell?"
"Will you endure what it takes?"
"How much are you actually willing to suffer?"
"How many times will you fail flat on your face in front of the world?"

Resistance is just a part of the process.
It's baked into the path to greatness.

Persistence in the boring, the mundane, and the unsexy over long periods of time without recognition is the cost of mastery.

If you look beyond the surface of anyone that has sustained excellence, not just flash in the pan 'success,' you will see a willingness to endure what most would never even consider.

99% of sustained excellence is simply a willingness to keep showing up with enthusiasm and conviction, no matter what. A willingness to keep getting punched in the face. A willingness to keep taking the gut shots and yet still show up the next day.

And the next. And the next. And the next. And the next. And the next. And the next. And the next. And the next.

I can tell you from experience that at the highest levels of special forces training, it isn't typically the physically or intellectually talented who make the cut. In fact, they're often the first to drop out. Why? Because their talent has often shielded them from having to develop the muscle to endure long after their body gives out.

But the 'non-talented', physically unimpressive scrappers who've been overlooked, counted out, and bypassed their entire lives? More often than not, they become the top soldiers on the planet. Because they'll simply endure more than anyone else. They have learned to never quit.

That's a trait you've been learning as well, and it will take you far in life."

Nakoma nodded, the mysterious chapters of Akira's life and wisdom always left her wanting more.

CHAPTER 14

A Life You Don't Need a Vacation From...

Iceland.

"Are you sure he'll be here?" Jonathan looked around and did not see many signs of life on the long and winding road. It sure looked like they were on their own.

Akira just nodded.

Sure enough, a few minutes later a lone Jeep appeared in the distance. As it got closer, they could see the SUV was covered in mud. A fit man about 6 feet 3 inches jumped out and engulfed the much smaller man in a bear hug. Akira introduced him, "Jonathan and Nakoma, this is the greatest living adventurer in this beautiful country! It is my pleasure to introduce you to 'Jon from Iceland.'"

"Great to meet you both!" Jon shook their hands, "I've heard a lot about you."

"Jon is one of the greatest adventurers in this country, which is saying something. He is an incredible human and one that that embodies an important principle: 'Create a life you don't need a vacation from.' He had been working a corporate job for a long time, and was adventuring in all his free time. Then one day after we met, he made the giant leap of faith and went all in on adventure and creativity. He now does creative work and adventure projects for big brands, traveling all over the world for them. My favorite thing about him though, is that he is a kind and curious human. We are fortunate, he doesn't often

57

take people on adventures with him, but he agreed to do me a favor and take us to a few of his favorite spots!"

They followed Jon down the highway, pulling off at a sign for a famous waterfall. But they weren't alone; two massive tour groups had just arrived, with big buses waiting and dozens of people milling around. The trail to the falls was already choked with foot traffic from other visitors.

Looking around, Jon shook his head. "It's a little crowded here. I have a better idea in mind."

Nakoma looked at him, curious. Jon said with a wink, "Someone we all love taught me, *there's always a back door.*" They all had a good chuckle and headed back to the vehicles.

They pulled back out onto the highway, driving away from the waterfall. Following the road higher up into the mountains, they drove for only a couple of minutes before Jon pulled off onto a smaller dirt road, following it to a dead end at a wooden fence.

They got out, looking around. There was no sign of anyone else, only two huge commercial warehouses, and no sign of a waterfall anywhere nearby, either. "This is the right spot?" Nakoma inquired, doubtful.

Jon grinned, nodded to a small ladder at the fence. "Sure it is. Like I said, there's always a back door."

They followed Jon over the ladder, where a tiny trail wound around the rocky hills. Five minutes later, Jonathan and Nakoma exchanged smiles: they could hear the roar of water rushing over stone. As they came around the bend in the trail, there it was in all its glory — an incredible waterfall thundered from the cliff face down into a huge pool.

"Not bad, right?" Jon smiled. Just like he'd said, there was no one else in sight. They were completely alone and got to enjoy the waterfall all to themselves.

* * *

"Jon, would you mind telling Nakoma about the philosophy of being kind and curious?" Akira asked when they got back to the vehicles and were changing out of their wet clothes.

"Absolutely! Every day my father told me and my brother to be kind and curious. He believed that if you embodied those two characteristics, they would carry you well in the world. In my experience, he was correct. They are two things that require no money, status, or special ability. Yet, they can open up people and the world around you in amazing ways!

So if at all possible — be kind and curious."

CHAPTER 15

Boiling the Frog

"Dad, you know you don't have to do that here."

Nakoma rolled her eyes as Jonathan climbed up a boulder to get a better photo. Mist hung thick across the valley below them, creating an undeniably picturesque landscape. It looked like something out of another world.

"Actually, I do. The marketing team was asking for more shots." Jonathan jumped off the boulder and joined Jon, Nakoma and Akira, who all stood there looking out over the massive tranquil lake, quietly absorbed in its raw natural beauty.

Nakoma shook her head, "Great. And then you'll obsess over posting the right one—"

"That's the job, honey. This life doesn't come free. Sometimes it takes a marketing partnership or two to pay for it all." Jonathan noticed Akira's face shift a bit. "What?"

"I've just never seen this side of you, that's all." You could hear the sadness in Akira's voice.

"To be fair, I wasn't running a business with global influence before." Jonathan fired back defensively.

"Ohhhhh, business. That's what that is?"

Jonathan nodded, explaining. "One of our sponsors is a nutrition company, I partnered with them on a new line of supplements. We launch at the end of the quarter."

"So now Dad has to do a partner post every week, instead of just enjoying the world's most incredible country with us," Nakoma pointed out.

Jonathan shrugged it off. "A lot of people depend on me for this, and it pays the bills. It's just business, honey."

"Is it, though?" Akira fixed Jonathan with a look that he knew well, and suddenly he felt a little self-aware, almost guilty. "I'm not so sure, Jonathan. It seems your priorities might be a little out of touch. If a teenager is telling you that you are spending too much time obsessing over a post, that is a pretty big tell."

Jonathan's face reddened. Nakoma grilled him often about how much time he obsessed over social media posts and comments. It was a strange role reversal to most parent-child relationships.

"I'm spending time with you right now—" Jonathan quickly retorted.

"Your eyes have spent more time on that screen than on the beauty in front of us. And you've been distracted all morning."

"Because I have a business to run. I don't necessarily want to do that, but I have to."

"Says who?" Akira looked at him, "Jonathan, you are immensely talented, incredibly well-trained and highly skilled. You don't *have* to do any of this. Not to mention the only two things you *have* to do in life are die and pay taxes.

We love you, and it just feels like you have become a little out of touch with yourself.

Have you watered down what sets your soul on fire to serve your business reputation and bank account? I know at times in my life I felt this happening to me, and I had to make some drastic changes to make sure I wasn't a boiling frog."

Nakoma snorted a laugh, "A boiling frog?!"

"Do you know how you boil a frog, Nakoma?"

She chuckled, thinking aloud, "I take it, you don't just put it in boiling hot water?"

"Nope! The way you boil a frog alive, is by putting it in warm water, and then slowly increasing the temperature. Degree by degree, the water warms, but the frog doesn't feel it, until it's too late. If we aren't careful, this happens to us over time. Lots of little choices eventually transform us into a person who is very far from who we started as.

Sometimes, this is the exact beautiful transformation, evolution, and growth we are looking for. But it can work both ways: those tiny choices can also transform us into a shadow of ourselves, who is no longer aligned with our truest and most authentic self."

For a moment, the only sound was the majestic thunder of another of Iceland's waterfalls. Jonathan's brow wrinkled as he processed Akira's correction.

Sensing his internal conflict, Nakoma chimed in gently, "Dad, I love you so much. I know how lucky I am to be your daughter. You're amazing, flaws and all — it is ok and honestly refreshing when people are authentic, even on social media. The pressure from everyone expecting perfection through filters, angles, and acting like everything is perfect all the time, it gets exhausting. And I don't like seeing it affect you like this."

Jonathan sighed, "I'm sorry, honey. To be honest, I didn't realize the effects it had on me. From now on, I'm making a commitment to be more present with you guys and less worried about everything else."

CHAPTER 16

Paradoxes of Life

Tigray, Ethiopia.

Sweat poured across Nakoma's face as she knelt before the tiny trickle of water the villagers referred to as a 'stream'. She lowered a cracked plastic scoop into the cloudy liquid, then emptied it into the massive plastic can (the locals called it a 'jerry can') that she would use to bring the water back up the hill. Scoop by scoop, she filled it.

"Ready to go?" Across from her, Jonathan had just finished filling his own can. Nakoma nodded, then fit her arms under the fabric loops that functioned as straps. Wearing the can like a backpack, she stood and followed her father as they began their trek back up the steep hill.

They'd only landed yesterday, and were now in the middle of nowhere as far as Nakoma could tell. Around them, the sun beat down relentlessly. Clouds of flies buzzed in the air, and the smell of fuel, animal dung, and burning trash lingered like a haze. This was a very different world from the spotless, cold streets of Switzerland, and the mostly uninhabited fjords of Iceland.

Thirty minutes of hard hiking later, they reached the collection of shacks and huts that made up the tiny farm village at the top of the hill. Nakoma unloaded her water, exhausted. As she caught her breath, she heard a familiar voice.

"Well, what do you think?" She turned to see Akira approaching them, trailed by another man with salt-and-pepper hair.

Jonathan smiled, shaking the second man's hand. "That hike is longer than I remember, Scott."

"A lot changes in a decade, and that's a good thing!" Scott replied, indicating a gleaming metal well in the center of the village. A few children took turns pumping clean, fresh water from it, laughing and playing. "No one in this village has had to make that hike in a year, thanks to our new well. It's changed their lives."

Scott Harrison and his organization, *Charity Water*, had made it their mission to provide clean drinking water to the continent of Africa. And over the past decade, they started making good on that mission, rallying over 1 million people to help as they dug 78,000+ wells and water projects to provide clean water to millions.

"I'm thirsty," Nakoma admitted, wiping the sweat from her forehead.

"Then get a drink — as long as it isn't from there," Akira indicated her jug. "That water contains parasites that could give you a dozen illnesses almost immediately."

Nakoma registered that, amazed. "How did all these people survive, drinking that?"

"Many didn't," Scott replied. "In fact, contaminated water is how that happens."

Across the square, an older man struggled to drink from his water bottle. A web of scar tissue split his mouth, curling up onto his cheek, which was caved unnaturally inward. "That's my friend Tadele. He got NOMA when he was a teenager. It's a gangrenous flesh-eating bacteria that is widely found in contaminated water. We were able to stop it before it killed him, but he'll carry the scars for life. Many weren't as lucky."

Nakoma nodded. Since she'd arrived in Africa, she'd been registering the vast differences in daily life here. So many things she took for granted during her normal daily life — working cars, phones, electricity, widely available food and water — were luxuries that were far from guaranteed here. It was enough to make her dizzy.

"It's refreshing, isn't it?" Akira didn't seem to be feeling the same way. In fact, ever since they landed, the old man had barely stopped smiling. "Every time I visit this place, I am reminded of what's truly important in life. There are over one billion people on the planet that do not have access to clean drinking water. That number is dropping because of *Charity Water's* work, but there are still so many people in the world that lack access to basic necessities.

Every time I am here, and I see the joy that these people exhibit while having so little in terms of opportunities, healthcare, and basic human needs, I am reminded that even on my worst days, I am incredibly blessed.

When your day feels overwhelming, when you look around and see many people with more opportunities and resources, when life doesn't feel fair, take a moment and meditate on the fact that millions of people are currently praying for the 'terrible' circumstances you find yourself in. When you are in the heat of battle and the pressure feels like it is too much, remember that pressure is *the* privilege and at one point you would have given anything to be in the position you are now in."

CHAPTER 17

David Before Goliath

Negev Desert.

Nakoma had never seen a place so desolate. Endless dunes of rose-colored sand stretched out under the blazing sun, like an ocean that shimmered in the heat. The place seemed extraterrestrial, like it existed outside of our planet's time and space.

She wiped sweat from her eyes. Climbing the dune was exhausting; the sand sucked her feet down, making each step take the same work as four or five steps on firmer ground. She shifted her sandboard from one arm to the other and kept climbing, finally reaching the top of the ridge where Akira waited for her.

He hit a stopwatch. "You made it! Faster than your last run, too."

Hands on her knees, Nakoma gasped for air. "Ugh… these sand dunes are no joke!"

Despite the punishing physical toll of climbing massive sand dunes all day, this was her own idea. She knew that if she slacked on her conditioning, her performance at the X Games would suffer. And when she wasn't able to get in the gym or on the slopes — like today — that meant taking advantage of what she had: like sand dunes.

"I'm proud of you, Nakoma. You're doing something that King David did in this very desert thousands of years ago."

Nakoma had heard of King David, but knew very little about him. "Really? What is that?"

"Being faithful with the little things that are in your hand." Akira scanned the horizon, as if imagining what it was like a few thousand years before. "Long before he became King of Israel, David was a shepherd to a small flock of sheep.

No matter what came his way, David was faithful in tending sheep.
He was faithful in protecting those sheep.
He was willing to lay down his life for his sheep.
He killed lions and bears without modern weapons. All he had was his staff and his slingshot. Think about how crazy that is! We often read stories like that and glaze over it. Can you imagine defending a flock of sheep with nothing but a stick and a slingshot from BEARS and LIONS?!"

For a moment, Nakoma did exactly that. As her imagination exploded with the images that flashed across it, she shook her head, eyes wide, "NO! Absolutely not!"

"Often times our greatest opportunities are disguised as these tiny but monumental decisions of whether or not we will be faithful, and sometimes in crazy circumstances.

There is another story that only has one line in the ancient book about the man who would become King David's chief bodyguard. *He chased a lion down into a pit on a snowy day and killed it.**

Most people would constitute ending up in a pit with a lion on a snowy day the worst of days, but for Benaiah, it became all he needed on his resume. When David heard of his feats, he made him his chief bodyguard. David had intimate experience with the courage and skill it took to do what Benaiah had done.

David is remembered for killing Goliath, but the reason he was prepared and ready for his 'Goliath moment' is that he had been ridiculously faithful in this desert tending and defending sheep for years beforehand.

Whenever we become faithful with what's in our hand, when we become faithful with what feels like little sheep, what we may not realize is that it's actually building and refining our character so that when those Goliath opportunities come, we can step up to the plate with *conviction* like David and Benaiah did. Not confidence, not feelings that come and go, but with *conviction* — which can only be earned through years of preparation by protecting the little things, preparing with the little things, and being faithful to the little things.

Everyone thinks they want the opportunities under the bright lights, but those lights are so bright that they reveal everything from our faithfulness or lack thereof in the dark. Our responsibility is to be incredibly faithful tending our little sheep, and a willingness to fight the lions in our life, so that when the opportunities of our dreams do come, we are able to operate with pure conviction.

Our fate in those moments is determined long before, based off of our willingness or unwillingness to suffer and do the dirty work that feels insignificant and meaningless at the time."

Nakoma nodded, Akira's words hitting her heart. She knew she had Goliath moments coming and needed to prepare now more than ever.

*Awesome book, *In A Pit With A Lion On A Snowy Day*, by Mark Batterson

CHAPTER 18

Dancing in the Rain

Manuel Antonio, Costa Rica.

Jonathan blinked through blinding rain, frustrated and soaked to the bone. An hour ago, they'd all been gazing out over an endless horizon of jungle from a mountaintop vista. A thunderclap later, he knew the storm would be there soon, and he was right.

By the time they were halfway down the mountain, that thunderstorm hadn't let up. In fact, it seemed even more powerful, nearly reaching monsoon strength, even drenching through their 'waterproof' jackets. But while Jonathan couldn't hide his frustration, shaking the water off his back, Nakoma just laughed and took off her jacket instead — holding her arms wide, allowing the drops of rain to splash the sweat off her skin. She ran around with her tongue out, catching rain drops on it like snowflakes, laughing.

Seeing her joy, Akira smiled and began pulling off his own jacket. Jonathan looked at them flabbergasted. "What are you guys doing?! You are crazy!"

"Maybe we are!" Akira laughed as he and Nakoma were now in full dance mode. "It's been too long since I got to dance in a storm!"

Jonathan just shook his head as Akira and Nakoma did an impromptu spin move, twirling along together. Nakoma held out her hand, pulling Jonathan into it. After a moment, he couldn't resist smiling and dancing along.

He had to admit: the fresh rain felt great after their difficult hike. Eventually, Nakoma's joy was infectious enough to change Jonathan's attitude and they were all having a rain dance party.

* * *

Later, they were enjoying an afternoon espresso on the balcony of their home for the night. Around them, it was still raining 'rainforest hard.' Akira looked upward and smiled. "Isn't it amazing, Jonathan? A few thousand feet above us, there's nothing but, bright blue sky, and fluffy white clouds. We all know it; we see it every time we take off in an airplane. Despite the fact that down here the world is dark, wet and tumultuous, up there it's a glorious day…

It's just a reminder that even in the darkest storm, the sun is still shining on the other side of the clouds. No matter what storm you're in, it will eventually pass — even though there's nothing you can do to make it pass any faster.

So, what will you do with your time in the storm?

Will you succumb to frustration and get angry about it? Or, will you dance through it like Nakoma showed us today? No matter the storm, we always have the option.

Tomorrow may suck.
Tomorrow may bring heart break.
Tomorrow may be awful.

Does that mean we should throw away the possible joy of this moment because there could possibly be misery in the tomorrow? Does that mean we should squander the opportunities and joy from today?

Worry doesn't add much value to anything.

Prepare for the worst if you must, but be at least be grateful, fully present, and love what you have now. Because more often than not you'll look back — even after the pain, and anger, and humiliation — and wish you had at least enjoyed it and danced the rain.

If it rains, dance in it.

If the sun is out, dance in it.

Only you get to choose if you dance in spite of your circumstances and what may come.

Whatever comes doesn't have to stop us from enjoying what we have now.

This is why, when obstacles and challenges arrive in my life, I've trained myself to lean on two simple responses.

"Thank You," and *"Good."*

No matter what life throws at us, those responses never fail.

"Thank you."

"Good."

The mindset behind each is the same: treating every setback as the opportunity to become greater. Why *wouldn't* you be grateful for that?!

Gratitude is a superpower and secret weapon. It opens us to possibilities we cannot see when we allow our amygdala to run the show.

Play offense, not just defense.

We are conditioned to go to the doctor when we get sick, but we also need to do the work in advance to enable our own flourishing and health, not be solely dependent on doctors treating us once we're finally sick.

Gratefulness prayer.
Mindfulness training.
Meditation.
Beneficial and constructive self-talk.

All of these tools help us observe the storms, instead of being consumed by them. These skills allow us to choose the superpower of gratitude when life is throwing blows.

Even in the wildest storms, these tools allow our consciousness to rise above our circumstances to where the sun is shining on the other side.

This storm too shall pass.

Will you dance in the rain, or complain about it?

Often when we look back, it is the hard stuff we overcame that we remember the most fondly. Winning is cool, but the memories we make with the muck life throws at us are the ones that contain the most joy. Nakoma will win many gold medals, but many decades from now, us dancing in the rain will mean more than those. I promise you that."

As if to underscore this point, a massive thunderclap echoed through the jungle, punctuating the peaceful rainfall. Jonathan smiled, "Sounds like God agrees with you!"

CHAPTER 19

The Choice

Sanya Slum, Tokyo. The Past.

After three weeks, 8-year-old Akira knew he was alone for good this time.

His parents had a tough life marred by addiction and poverty beforehand, but the loss of a child had pushed them into the abyss.

His father often disappeared for days on end, drinking away his small earnings in the shadowy hovels that passed as bars in their sprawling slum on the edges of Tokyo City. And his mother wasn't much better, her life moving in a similar addict's rhythm — gone for days, only to return when she briefly sobered up.

Not that his life improved much when they *were* around. Akira had learned at an early age how fast he needed to be to escape his father's drunken rages, though he still carried scars from the nights when he sacrificed his own body to protect his baby brother.

Knowing he was now completely alone in the world, bone-deep hunger had driven him beyond their shanty town, and further into the city. He survived there for months, learning quickly that no one cared about another child orphaned to Tokyo's streets. But he also learned that most people wouldn't even look at one — and when you're a starving child in a big city, that can be an advantage.

It was just another day when he slipped into the butcher's shop just behind another shopper, waiting until the man was ordering to duck around the counter. Akira had always been quick, and his reflexes were sharpened by surviving on the streets — so stealing the half-chicken wasn't difficult, nor was dodging the butcher who spotted and chased him.

No, it was the policeman coming around the corner as he was fleeing the shop.

Still, he had come to know the city better than the law did — and in fact, he had already walked through his escape route earlier that day, just in case. It paid off now, as he scrambled through a tiny gap of fencing, leaving the officer in his dust, ignoring his shrieking whistle and shouts of "Stop! Thief!" as Akira sprinted off with his meal.

It wasn't until he made it all the way back to his shanty that Akira finally relaxed. He tore into the chicken, every bite better than the last, until —

"What is your name, boy?"

The deep voice startled him, and Akira realized that he hadn't heard a sound as the man approached. But now he stood in the doorway, outlined in sunlight. Akira could see his eyes were deep-set and sharp, sparkling with strength and understanding. Unlike the rough worker's garb or dark suits worn by the city's salarymen, he wore traditional robes — simple but elegant, as if he had walked out of another century.

"My name is Akira," Akira fought to keep his voice from shaking.

"Nice work with the chicken, Akira. That was quite an escape.

Don't worry, I am not here to harm you or turn you in. Do you have a family, or are you on your own?" Akira somehow knew he could trust this strange man. So he told him the truth — that he was an orphan, a hungry one. The man nodded, then fixed Akira with a piercing look.

"Akira, my name is Toshiro Yamashita, and I can help you have a very different and better life. If you come with me, you will never go hungry. Your life will still be hard, just a very different kind of hard. You will have to trust me and do exactly as I say.

The choice is yours, do you want a new life?

* * *

Costa Rica. The Present.

When he woke up from the dream, Akira was sweating through his sheets. He calmed a bit as he remembered that day — one that had changed his life forever. As he took a drink from the water glass at his bedside, he breathed deeply, grateful for the thousandth time that on that day, despite his fear and the uncertainty, he had answered, "Yes."

CHAPTER 20

"Terminal"

"Nakoma, honey. Have you seen Akira?"

Rain drummed on the roof. Jonathan had just clocked out of his final call of the day, and found his daughter buried in a book — but there was no sign of Akira. She stirred, barely looking up. "He went to take a nap, I think."

But Jonathan couldn't find him in the bedroom, and the office was empty as well. "Akira!" Jonathan heard a rustle in the bathroom and knocked on the door. "Akira?"

His mentor's voice seemed weaker than usual. "Come in, Jonathan."

Jonathan was startled to find Akira sitting on the floor, head dropped into his hands. His face was pale, and he did nothing to hide the fact that he was clearly in pain.

"Are you okay?"

Akira grimaced a bit as he massaged his temples. His eyes were shut tightly, like he was trying to keep the light out of them. "Well, that depends on your definition of 'okay'."

"Can I get you anything? Tylenol or something?" Akira couldn't help but chuckle. "Jonathan, my dear friend… Tylenol won't help what I have. No medicine has."

Jonathan hesitated. Afraid to hear the answer, even as he asked, "Why not?"

With a deep breath, Akira looked into Jonathan's eyes and replied gently, "I have glioblastoma, Jonathan. Brain cancer. There are three inoperable tumors in my brain that are growing very aggressively. When they press on my optic nerve, it makes every other moment of pain I've ever experienced before feel like a light massage. So no, Tylenol isn't going to help."

Brain cancer. His words hit Jonathan like a knockout punch. He instantly found it hard to breathe, barely able get the words out, "Is it... I mean, are you, you know...?"

"Am I terminal?" Akira nodded gently. "Like I told you before, Jonathan: the only guarantee in life, is death. <u>We're all terminal</u>."

"They can't do anything at all?"

"Oh, certainly. They showed me a list of options, each of them more damaging and life-destroying than the last. Poison. Radiation. It might extend my life for a while, sure. But what kind of life would it be? Trapped in a bed, dying slowly.

I've always known that I have a limited amount of time in this world, and it appears it is now more limited than ever. I tried to keep it from you as long as I could, so that it wouldn't hang heavy over our time together, but as soon as I got the diagnosis, that's when I sent for you. The 'treatment' I chose was a month of global adventures with my two favorite people. I haven't known a living blood relative for over sixty years — and the two of you are closer to me than any family member ever was.

* * *

She's taking it better than I am, thought Jonathan. He watched as Akira explained everything to Nakoma. She didn't say anything at first, just wiped away a tear and then gave him a huge long squeeze as the tears started flooding down all their faces.

I guess I shouldn't be surprised, Jonathan thought. As long as he'd known the old sensei, Akira had lived in a way that seemed to defy normal life expectations. Even now, in the face of death, that fact remained unchanged. Jonathan realized now what an incredible gift it was for him and Nakoma to be with Akira during this time.

Jonathan was struggling though, and he excused himself to the restroom. Once alone, all the emotions started to overwhelm him. It felt like he couldn't breathe. His chest was so tight.

It all felt like too much.

He had been doing his best to raise Nakoma on his own while managing the mountain of stress he faced at work with the acquisition, but now this? This just felt like too much. He sat by himself and grieved for over an hour.

CHAPTER 21

Social Circle

The weight Jonathan felt the moment he heard Akira's diagnosis hadn't let up. In fact, it had only gotten worse and it seemed as if an impossibly heavy blanket was on his shoulders. Try as he might to be strong for Nakoma and Akira, Jonathan was emotionally and psychologically broken. He was tired of opening his heart and having it shattered.

The next couple of days he was withdrawn, even while Nakoma and Akira seemed to grow that much closer. It was as if the news made them even more determined to pack as much fun, laughter and light as possible into the time they had together. They seemed to be having an even better time, playing games, going for walks, and shopping.

Nakoma was wise beyond her years and had her mother's intuition, so she and Akira hatched a plan to try and help her father.

When Jonathan's wife passed away, one of his best friends stepped up and became a rock in Nakoma's world. Tonja was the kind of person that everyone loved and wanted to be around. She had that special ability to make someone feel loved and invincible at the same time.

* * *

When they pulled into Social Circle, Georgia, Jonathan finally figured out who they were going to see. He had coached Tonja's son, Ben, when he was pitching at Georgia Tech.

Jonathan had finished writing *Chop Wood Carry Water* at that time, so naturally, Tonja was one of the first people to know about it and read it.

She became one of the book's greatest champions and Jonathan knew she was singlehandedly the biggest factor in why it went viral. She had lovingly encouraged *everyone* in her company to read it. Within a year, it had become like the Bible for their entire global organization.

While Jonathan was incredibly grateful for that, all of that paled in comparison to the value of her friendship and the love she showered on him and Nakoma.

Finally alone with Tonja in her living room, Jonathan unloaded. Tears flowing and chest heaving, the emotion flowed out of him. *"I don't want to invest anymore and open my heart to more heartbreak. I have already experienced too much pain. I just can't… I can't take it."*

Tonja teared up as well, her empathy wrapping around him like a hug. "Oh honey, boy do I understand and empathize with that perspective.... It is an option for sure."

Jonathan nodded. "I'm sure you explored that road after Bengie passed."

"I sure did, and for good reason. Bengie was my best friend for thirty-four years and as you know, he was one of the most incredible people to walk this earth. How lucky was I? I got to do life with him as business partners, as parents, and lovers for over three decades. We had a dream relationship. We had a dream family, with Sara and Ben who became superstar Division 1 athletes, and even better people. We always wanted to be together, and virtually always were. We didn't need the fancy things or fancy places that our hard work over many decades had afforded us the ability to have — all we ever wanted was each other. We got to go to some of the most incredible places on earth, but we were just as happy being here in our little town, because we had each other.

When he got sick, I went into overdrive to find the best medical care in the world, and we fought for a year and a half, fully believing that he would be healed, and this would be nothing but a bump in the road along our journey. So when he told us, 'I'm ready to go be with Jesus,' well…"

Tonja trailed off, a deep ragged breath reminding him of the grief she'd been through. "I wasn't ready or prepared. I had not let that possibility creep into my mind. I refused to believe anything but him having a full and total recovery.

I had some very dark times after that, and as you know, I went from being the life of every party and wanting to always be with people to being exhausted and frustrated by virtually everyone and seemingly everything.

The world wanted me to just move on and get over it, but I just wanted to scream, 'DON'T YOU REALIZE THE LOVE OF MY LIFE, THE MOST INCREDIBLE MAN IS GONE!! THIS ISN'T FAIR! HOW IS THE WORLD STILL MOVING FORWARD?!'

For a long time, I shut myself off to most people and to the world at large.

But that didn't fix anything.

Eventually I realized that I had two options. I could lament that my best friend was gone, and my life would never be the same, *or* I could focus on the fact that I was the luckiest person in the world.

I have never known another person who had a relationship like mine. People couldn't believe how perfect ours was, and I got that dreamy, better-than-Disney relationship for THIRTY-FOUR years! Many people would give anything to have that for a month or a year, and I got it for over three decades!"

Jonathan nodded, remembering just how special her marriage to Bengie was. To those who knew them, they were the perfect couple, whose incredible love for each other seemed to illuminate the lives of everyone around them.

Tonja sighed, her eyes filled with that same love even now. "Jonathan, we get to decide which perspective we lean into. The hard part is, both of them are true.

It's not easy." She deeply sighed. "It really sucks sometimes, but, I know that I always have the option to see beyond the storm.

We can choose to allow our pain to shut down our heart and kill our ability to love those around us, because that absolutely opens us up to more pain and heartache. OR, we can choose to lean in and love *even harder*, be *even more present*, and choose to go all in, because we know that any moment can be the last moment we get with someone.

Bengie was the epitome of health and strength, until he wasn't.

Just because someone looks healthy — or young — doesn't mean they're guaranteed more life; this is why I do my best every day to choose to love with abandon, and never pretend that anyone is going to get another day — another moment — because it's not promised. So, every day I do my best to choose, to lean in, open my heart, and love with reckless abandon."

Jonathan took a deep breath, realizing it was now a bit easier to breathe. The blanket of grief was still there, but it definitely felt a bit lighter. He gave Tonja a long hug, grateful for her wisdom — and the intuition of his own daughter, who had somehow known exactly what he needed, exactly when he needed it.

* * *

In bed a few hours later, Jonathan was peaceful and silent. Tonja's words repeated in his head. "—we can choose to love *even harder*, be *even more present*, and choose to go all in…"

Was he really going 'all in'? He thought about his life and what he'd experienced in the past few weeks with Akira and Nakoma. He knew what it was time to do.

Before falling asleep, he emailed his lawyer, halting his company's acquisition. Then he shut off his phone, closed his eyes, and slept better than he had in years.

CHAPTER 22

A New Mission

Lake Oconee, Georgia.

A couple days at Tonja's lake house were a nice time of rest and relaxation they all needed.

Once Nakoma went to bed, Jonathan and Akira were left alone. At first, Jonathan didn't speak, watching as Akira calmly poured two glasses of his favorite Japanese whiskey. They clinked glasses and each took a sip in silence.

As the fog of his own emotion had cleared, so had Jonathan's mind. Akira's words to him — *"I need your help with my final project"* — in fact, this entire strange worldwide journey he was taking them on — was illuminated in a brand-new light.

It all made sense now, and Jonathan was humbled by the fact that of all Akira's friends, he had chosen Jonathan and Nakoma to accompany him on this final journey: "So what is this final project that you need my help with?"

Akira reached into his travel bag, pulling out a beautiful journal. Its pages and cover looked like it had seen better days. But he held it with reverence, offering it to Jonathan as if it was a priceless relic. "My final project for you to finish, is a manuscript. I started working on it before the diagnosis, but it got to be too much. I knew that I needed your help. No one else can articulate my stories and wisdom the way you can. You have a special gift."

Jonathan took it graciously, and bowed, "Of course, I'll do my best to honor your life and wisdom."

"Do me a favor. Wait until I am gone to open it." Jonathan thought it was an odd request, but told Akira that he would respect his wishes.

"My true life's work is my relationships. This book, while I hope it impacts as many people as possible, is not my life's work. My real 'life's work' are the people I've been blessed to do life with. That's why I'm asking you to finish it: I've seen what you can do with the written word. Your story sharing our journey together as sensei and student touched many people around the world, and my hope is that — while the wisdom contained in these pages will be different — the impact might be similar. You are the only person I trust to make it come to life the way it is supposed to."

Akira grinned, that twinkle back in his eye, "Just don't mess it up. After all, it's only the last wish of your dying mentor."

Then he went stone-faced. Jonathan couldn't tell if he was serious or not, until — finally — he broke into laughter. Jonathan just shook his head, "Not funny." This, of course, just made Akira laugh harder, until Jonathan finally admitted with a small smile, "Okay… it's a little funny."

"It sure is," chuckled Akira. "But don't worry, I'm not dead yet! And while I'm still here, we still have places to go, and people to see."

Jonathan nodded. "You're the boss. Where are we going next?"

Akira's smile was tired, but still as bright as ever. "Next, we are going to my favorite spot on Earth! I just got word that an order

I placed a few weeks ago with some old friends is finally ready to be picked up."

CHAPTER 23

Owning Things vs. Things Owning You

Capri, Italy.

The house was tucked away from a thin cobblestone road that wound along high cliffs. Its old wooden door looked like all the others on the street: cracked blue paint, set into the smooth white plaster walls, and covered in climbing green ivy.

Akira took a deep breath as he approached the door. With effort, he raised the door knocker and let it fall a few times, the deep thump echoing. A moment later, the door cracked open. Akira greeted the middle-aged woman who answered, speaking briefly in Italian with her before she broke into a big grin, speaking excitedly as she opened the door to allow them inside. They stepped through, entering one of the most beautiful courtyards Jonathan had ever seen.

The villa around them was simple, its architecture timeless and beautiful. Whitewashed plaster walls covered in ivy and flowers. Nakoma inhaled the fragrances deeply, there were delightful hints of lemon and jasmine from the nearby gardens.

Jonathan couldn't help but let out a low whistle, impressed. "This place is unreal," he murmured, his gaze sweeping from the sparkling waters up to the towering cliffs.

"Oh, it's real," replied Akira. "Long ago, this was my dream home."

Nakoma was stunned, "You lived here?!"

"I dreamed about it for years before finally being able to buy it. Then, yes, I lived here, for some of the happiest years of my life," the old man nodded. "I even built that archway. I designed it for this time of day, too. Best view on the island."

Sure enough, the view through the courtyard's arch was spectacular. Its weathered stones framed the sun as it dropped into the ocean, igniting the sky in strokes of orange, pink, and purple. For a moment, they all just stood there, hypnotized by the view.

Then Jonathan stirred, "If I lived here, I don't think I'd ever leave. Why did you?"

"Because instead of me owning this house, the house began to own me. Too often we think that we own things, but they actually own us. I love this place, and Capri is still one of, if not my favorite spot in the world, but one home is more than enough for me.

At one point I owned three homes: Tokyo, here, and San Diego. I thought I was living my best life, but it was my sweet late wife who pointed out to me that those homes actually owned me. I was constantly focused on repairs, the upkeep — and the taxes, Lord almighty, the taxes! Trash, water, landscaping, painting, and so many other things. Then when she wanted to travel somewhere new, I always shut it down, because we were spending so much on these places, we actually became anchored to them.

It stopped when she took a trip by herself because I "needed to check on the place.' On the third day by myself, I called an agent and put it on the market. I sold my apartment in San Diego the same year. My wife was my home, and I never wanted to travel without her. I made a commitment to never let things own me again."

Surveying the view, Akira grinned. "Now, that isn't to say we ought to live like monks all our lives. There's a lot to be said for appreciating mastery, which can be found at the heart of plenty of beautiful things. With that in mind, let's go take a walk into town."

CHAPTER 24

A Perfect Fit

A kira led them through the streets of Capri, along a maze of cobbled pathways that twisted and turned past gardens and sunlit piazzas. They passed rows of shops offering artisanal crafts, fine linens, and handcrafted jewelry, finally reaching an impressive storefront with bold red lettering spelling out *ISAIA*.

Nakoma noticed a few suits on display in the windows. Akira posed in front of the store with his arms spread wide, "ISAIA, my favorite brand in the world, and this is their flagship store."

Inside, they found an elegant space that looked more like a classy lounge or cool bar than a tailoring shop. A smiling Italian man in a trim custom suit greeted them, his face lighting up, "Akira! It has been too long my friend! Julia told me you were coming in for a special order, so I made sure to clear my schedule."

Akira embraced him warmly, introducing him to Jonathan and Nakoma. "This is Gianluca, one of the world's greatest living tailors. He turns simple fabric and thread into wearable works of art. ISAIA is a small family brand, and when I started giving keynotes around the world, my dear friend Seth Mattison, who was very established in the speaking world, advised that I should invest in a piece. Over time I accumulated many of their suits, and personally know many of the staff in their boutiques around the world. Seth and I even did a workshop for a group at their beautiful Beverly Hills store many years ago."

Gianluca gestured to the back of the store. "Your pieces are ready, if you'd like to see them. Julia can't wait to meet you all!"

He ushered them into the back room, which was stepping into the heart of a craftsman's studio. Pieces of suits in various stages hung from mannequins, each stitch a testament to the tailor's skill and attention to detail. Drawers overflowing with colorful silk linings and cashmere swatches, tables stacked with gleaming scissors and rolls of exquisite fabrics.

Julia saw them coming and lit up, greeting Nakoma first. "Oh my goodness! This must be the angel you have told me so much about?! You are even more beautiful than Akira described! It is so great to finally meet you."

Nakoma blushed, and while she knew that she was good looking, her dad always told her that looks were not earned and shouldn't be given much value. So, she got a little shy anytime someone was in awe of her looks. She instead preferred to wow them with her work ethic, wisdom and kindness. She quickly changed the subject away from herself, "So, all of this is just to make suits?"

Julia half frowned, before chuckling, "Oh honey, these are not 'just suits.' These are more like a superhero's cape. When an ordinary person puts one on, they feel invincible, but when a special person puts it on, they *become* invincible!" She winked, knowing she was only half lying. There was something about an ISAIA suit that could make people tap into a greater version of themselves, especially on stages doing the one thing most of the world would rather die than do.

Gianluca presented two beautifully crafted custom suits. But when Akira tried on the first one, the suit swallowed him. Jonathan and Nakoma tried to hide their embarrassment, as

Nakoma quipped, "I think you might have lost a little weight since you gave them your measurements."

As everyone laughed, Jonathan couldn't help but sneak in a jab, "And you might have shrunk as well!"

Akira's mischievous grin returned, "Maybe *you* should try it on!"

Jonathan was confused at first, but Akira insisted. And sure enough, when he came out from behind the curtain — the suit fit him like a glove. He rolled his eyes and shot Akira a look. "I can't believe you did this…"

The suit was a sharp, timeless cut in the famous Capri blue with the notorious ISAIA red pin on the lapel. "Of course I did!" His old mentor grinned.

"How did you know my measurements?!"

"I got them from your assistant, and Gianluca and Julia did the rest. Now let's see yours on you, Nakoma!"

The second suit was a softer, elegantly tailored piece in light gray with subtle hints of bright teal stitching through the accents — Nakoma's favorite color. She was shocked. She usually wore more street style and athletic clothing, but she had to admit — this suit looked incredibly sharp.

A few minutes later, both she and Jonathan stood in front of the group with huge grins. Both suits fit perfectly, the tailoring offering the same comfort and freedom of movement as a pair of sweats — all while boasting style ready to walk a red carpet.

"Made to measure, as we call it, is crafted not only to fit the body but to match the essence of its wearer," Gianluca explained with a proud nod, watching them admire themselves in the full-length mirrors. "Akira shared a few details I took the liberty of including."

Nakoma turned to Akira, her eyes shining with gratitude. "Thank you!" Akira's color was fully back in his face for the first time in a week. Julia handed him two beautiful bright red hangers that were thicker and nicer than any Nakoma had ever seen. On each, both her and Jonathan's full names were embossed.

"My blessing!" he replied to Nakoma, handing her a hanger. "Each one also includes a little message from me. Check your inside pockets."

Sure enough, the inside pocket of each suit beautifully embroidered. On one side was their initials, and the other, two words: *FINISH EMPTY.*

CHAPTER 25

The Map is Not the Territory

"Nakoma, are you sure we're on the right path?"

Jonathan scanned the countryside around them. After being dropped off on a remote trailhead an hour ago, they should have reached the coast by now.

Nakoma checked her phone. "Yes. My service is kind of spotty here, but I think we're pretty close. At least, we *should* be…"

"According to what?" Asked Akira.

"Everyone who's posted from there. See?" She showed them a series of social media posts featuring a massive coastal waterfall, all geotagged on a map. "It's one of the most popular spots in this area, I don't think they *all* posted the wrong location —"

Akira looked from the map on her phone to the afternoon sun. "Sometimes technology isn't as reliable as nature," he said. "Could I see that, please?"

Comparing the map on Nakoma's phone to the landscape around them, Akira noted the position of the sun. Then he adjusted the angle of his watch, using its dial as a makeshift compass. "The coast is southeast of us, but this trail is leading us north. It's three o'clock, and the hour hand on my watch points east, so the coast is this direction." He pointed confidently, indicating a path that veered away from their current route.

Jonathan nodded, knowing better than to second-guess Akira's orienteering expertise.

Nakoma's face fell. "Okay, I think you're right. I think we got lost."

Jonathan's face twisted. "*WE, got lost?*"

Nakoma sighed, realizing what she'd done: even in how she'd phrased her sentence, she had ducked taking responsibility for her actions — something that Jonathan had always instilled in her. *Linguistic intentionality,* a phrase he had coined, was of huge importance in their family.

"You're right, Dad. I'm sorry. *I,* got lost, and because I insisted on leading us, I'm responsible for that." She looked at Akira, apologetic: "This will mean a longer hike. Is that okay?"

Akira just smiled, "As long as I am with you guys, I will be fine. Besides, this whole scenario reminds me of a lesson your father also had to learn the hard way years ago."

Jonathan chuckled, "The map is not the territory. In this case, literally."

As they began hiking again, Nakoma asked, "Can you explain that further for me?"

"Well, the map you were given to reach your destination — the waterfall — was faulty," Akira explained. "When you arrived here, it didn't match the territory. The same is true for many things in life."

Jonathan nodded in fierce agreement, "I would say this principle has only become more valuable since you first taught it to me. In fact, it seems like many of the maps we have been given were incredibly skewed."

"Like what?" Nakoma asked.

"Like the food pyramid, for example. My entire generation was raised to believe that the food pyramid was a trustworthy and valuable 'map' created through methodical research, meant to guide us toward healthier lives.

It turns out, the food pyramid wasn't made to guide citizens to eat healthier; it was created to promote the interests of several powerful food industry lobbyists. It was literally a marketing ploy dressed up as authoritative, scientific guidance — without any regard for the incredible damage it would do to the lives of countless people who accepted it as fact simply because it was promoted by government agencies.

Akira nodded gravely. "Never forget that doctors — paid by the tobacco lobby — recommended smoking as beneficial for health back in the day as well.

Or that even now, the 'pharmaceutical industrial complex' responds to illness with a prescription for whichever new pill one of the billion-dollar companies produces, instead of helping patient's baseline health habits like exercise, hydration, nutrition, sunshine, and sleep.

Of course, this isn't to say that all modern medicine is ineffective or compromised. It simply serves as a strong reminder to think critically about the 'maps' we are given in our lives, and how they may not match the territory of reality."

Jonathan went on, "Once you see this, you start to see it *everywhere*. It's shocking how often it's only incentives that drive the maps being handed out in our culture."

Akira nodded and chimed in, "When you pull back the curtains in a lot of industries — even religions — you realize that reality offers a very different territory than the maps they are providing.

Back to the pharmaceutical industry: if your business is sickness, what value is a healthy person to you? In the west you have sick care, not *health* care.

If your business is the military industrial complex and weapons manufacturing, what value is a peaceful world?

Again, that doesn't mean there aren't valuable maps. The map I received from Akira, for example, has changed my life and been critical to every success I've enjoyed. But I've learned to examine and think deeply about the incentives behind all the maps out there.

Here, look at this map. He opened a picture for her to see on his phone. "This is the map of the world you have probably been shown your whole life, and THAT is the actual size and scale of all the countries in the dark blue."

Nakoma shockingly inhaled, "No way!! Russia is three times bigger on the map we have all seen, and look how big Africa actually is?!"

"Strange, right?" Akira quipped. "Remember, no matter what people or governments say, the two things that drive their decisions are Money and Power. No matter whether it is Democracy or Socialism, Democrat or Republican, at the core is money and power.

Politicians and political parties do not care about you. They care about money and power. They change stances and positions anytime it suits them. They are as slimy and shape shifting as they need to be to keep the money and power flowing.

News organizations are not around to inform you objectively. They are driven by ratings and financial incentives. They will show you a version of the world that keeps you coming back for more, even if it distorts your perception of the world in harmful ways. Everyone has an agenda. Especially those that insist on telling you how fair, objective, and independent they are. It is wise to listen and watch many different sides, and then still think critically about all the information (maps) you've been presented, while knowing there are perspectives and sides to issues (the territory) you have still never heard.

People in the west laugh at the obvious propaganda from the east but are under the hypnosis of the three letter agencies influences from the greatest propaganda machine the world has ever known: HOLLYWOOD."

Akira stopped his diatribe and paused, sniffing the air. "I think we're close."

Sure enough, as they rounded the next bend, a majestic view appeared. The Italian coast stretched wide for miles above the ocean, and just up the trail… a majestic waterfall fed into the sea far below.

CHAPTER 26

Courage

Amalfi Coast, Italy.

"I don't know if I can do it, Dad." Nakoma leaned over the rocky cliff, staring down at the pool of deep turquoise water far below. Around them, roaring white jets of water fell from the waterfall that spilled across the massive rock face.

"Really? You fly off half-pipes and jumps all the time."

"Yeah, but if I eat it on a jump, I wipe out in snow. If I miss this, there's a bunch of rocks." She peered out over the waterfall, looking at all the razor-sharp rocks. It was undeniably beautiful, but also undeniably dangerous. A single move in the wrong direction seemed like it could kill you.

"Okay. That's an understandable feeling. But I have to ask, Nakoma. Which voice are you listening to right now?"

Nakoma paused, annoyed. This was an exercise they'd repeated so often that it felt like muscle memory to her. In the same way the vertigo of flipping upside-down on a snowboard at forty miles per hour was familiar to her, the next words that came out of her mouth did so with all the automatic ease of an unshakable habit: "That's my external voice."

"And what does your internal whisper say?"

"*I can do hard things.*" Nakoma drew in a deep breath, noticing that Akira stood silently beside them, watching her.

After a moment, he spoke. "Nakoma, I am glad you are afraid."

Confused, Nakoma responded. "Huh? Really?"

Akira beamed, "YES! Without fear, you wouldn't have the chance to be courageous. You cannot have courage without fear. Because courage isn't *not* having fear. Instead, courage is learning to *lean into* the fear and act anyway. It's a willingness to get beat down and embarrassed, it's a willingness to look stupid. Yet, in spite of it all, a willingness to keep getting in the arena no matter what.

Courage is not an absence of fear the way we think it is supposed to be. It is staring fear in the face and saying, I will brave whatever is scaring me, no matter the potential cost.

Bravery is learning to embrace the emotions fear stirs up. There is no such thing as fearless when the consequences matter to us.

People hear *'the point of life is not to arrive safely at death'* and it resonates deep within their souls, yet they will turn around and continue to choose perceived safety over courage. They choose easy over right. They act in ways that sap their potential and trap them in ways they can only fully realize from their life looking backwards.

In the moment it doesn't feel big, it just feels like a little compromise, but over time? All those choices become a compromised life diluted by regrets.

And I don't know about you, but I've chosen to embrace living a life without regrets, for as long as I get to keep on living it."

Akira backed away from the edge, a calm smile on his weathered face.

"I am afraid too, and I am so grateful for this opportunity, because it gives me another chance to be courageous." He spread his arms wide, his chest rose as he inhaled a deep breath and held it for a second. Then, with determination, he walked forward and dropped off the edge. Dropping through the air, he splashed into the pool far below, surfacing a second later with a wide smile on his face, laughing like a kid on Christmas morning.

Jonathan could not help but shake his head. Akira always found more ways to inspire him.

Jonathan backed up, then launched himself out into the air, a few seconds later splashing into the crystal blue water below. Nakoma was next. She took a deep breath, Akira's words echoing in her mind: *Courage is a willingness to lean into the fear and act anyway.*

She took three deep breaths, just like she learned to do before she started one of her snowboarding routines. Each breath drove her fear down into her, settling deep in her stomach, a churning tension that refused to go away.

Choose to be courageous.
Lean into the fear.
Act anyway.

Repeating that a few times, Nakoma backed up, took a few running steps, and jumped — rocketing out away from the cliff's edge — then dropping like a rock as she whooped, adrenaline shooting through her — cannon-balling into the water, then bobbing to the surface to find Akira and Jonathan waiting for her, pure joy on their faces.

"Looked like a perfect 10 to us!"

CHAPTER 27

"Bloom in your own time"

35k ft above the Atlantic Ocean.

The week of adventures in the Amalfi Coast was incredible, but now they were getting very close to the X Games and needed to go back to California to spend a few days on the mountain with her team. Akira also told them he wanted to take them to a couple places in Southern California where he had once lived.

Nakoma blinked, jolted back to reality by a bump of turbulence. Out the airplane window, puffy white clouds piled high over the ocean as they journeyed to LAX.

Looking at the time, she realized 30 minutes had passed. She felt a pang of disappointment — she had been meaning to limit her time on social media for the past month, and had been doing a good job of it. Until now, at least. This was the first time in a while that she felt like been sucked into the abyss.

Looking up from his book, Akira noticed her disappointment. "Something wrong?"

"Well, I just… I went down the rabbit hole a little bit. Lost track of time."

"I noticed. But it's also the first time I've seen you do that in weeks. Most kids your age can barely tear themselves away from their phones for a few minutes. But you've been doing the opposite. You barely look at yours."

Nakoma hesitated. "There's a good reason for that. Millions of people know about the incident, and for months I've read awful things people have written and said about me. The memes are brutal. Dad's been awesome about it, but I still think... I don't know, maybe he just doesn't get it."

"What about me?" Akira asked. "Maybe I'll get it."

Nakoma smiled at that, "That's kind of you, but I'm not sure even you'd understand."

The old man just shrugged. "Try me. Maybe I will surprise you."

Akira just sat there, silent as she explained. Nakoma was certain he wouldn't get it. What would an octogenarian know about the pressures and pitfalls of a teenager's life? She had been in the media spotlight since she was barely out of diapers. How could he understand the pressure of a life under the scrutiny of the online mob?

But she was surprised to see tears forming in the old man's eyes as he reached out and took her hands firmly in his. Looking her in the eyes, Akira replied, "I'm so, so proud of you, Nakoma. You are braver than most adults I've ever met."

Nakoma shook her head, surprised. "Really? It doesn't feel that way sometimes, and I don't know if I'll ever get out from this. It will follow me forever."

"That may be true, but I know you well enough to know that one mistake will not define you. Your generation faces pressures that older generations will never understand. I can't imagine what you've had to deal with.

From the day you could walk, many of your steps were broadcast to the entire planet. From the day you could read, all of the world's knowledge — the good, the bad, and the ugly — was right there at your fingertips. From the day you could relate to another human being, much of the world's population was there on the other side of that screen, waiting to judge you, cheer you on, shame you, love you, or hate you.

The world enjoys building people up, but sometimes I think it is for the sick pleasure of eventually getting to tear them down and watch them burn.

With all that power at your fingertips, no wonder people your age have the highest occurrence of mental health issues ever faced in the history of mankind. The immediacy of the world you live in can shatter your psyche if you aren't ready for it or well-trained enough to manage it.

A single mistake can be broadcast to the entire planet, and it can feel like your life is over in an instant. If you misspeak or mis-state your opinion on something, it doesn't matter; those words are already recorded forever. And God forbid that you ever say something that contradicts the popular narrative — the mob will come at you faster than a medieval village with their torches and pitchforks out, ready to hunt you down for having the nerve to voice a contrary opinion.

I don't know how you do it. You're only 13 years old and you've faced issues that would have taken plenty of adults my age out of the game entirely!"

Nakoma felt her heart warm with gratitude. She'd never heard any adult get it, or even come close to understanding what she constantly went through. "Thank you."

"The truth is, Nakoma, I admire you greatly. You've chosen one of the most difficult things someone your age can choose to do: to live your life in the arena, instead of on the sidelines. When you choose life in the arena, you have a massive target on your back. On top of that — through social media — you have daily access to the top .000001% of the human race, along with their curated highlight reels. It's more difficult than ever to stay in the dark chasing excellence and focused only on what you can control.

Comparison is a deadly trap, and because of technology it is in our face the moment we open our phones. It effortlessly steals the joy from our work, joy that is needed fuel to unlock the greatness inside us."

Nakoma realized he was right; she regularly compared herself to the best snowboarders in the world — she followed all of them, sometimes obsessively watching their tricks and training. Seeing their progress had often pushed her to try bigger tricks, and she knew it made her feel worse when she couldn't land them. She also saw what all the other 'cool' girls and women from Paris, Hollywood, and beyond were doing, getting, where they were at, and who they were with.

"So what should I do, Akira? I can't help comparing myself sometimes."

"The answer," Akira smiled, "Is *oubaitori*. To 'bloom in your own time.'"

"What does that mean?"

"It's a concept that embodies the spirit of not comparing oneself to others. *Oubaitori* is often written with four kanji characters: 桜 梅 桃 李. Each character represents a different kind of blossom: cherry, apricot, peach and plum. They're all different, and each is remarkable in its own way, without needing comparisons.

But just like trees bloom differently, so do humans. We each pass through seasons of growth or seasons where it seems like nothing is happening — even if massive changes are happening beneath the surface, changes we aren't even aware of yet. But those seasons arrive at different times for everyone, which is why comparison is such a silly game. It can lead us to miss out on opportunities because we're focusing exclusively on what other people have done or how they look, instead of seizing the opportunity that's actually before us.

The idea behind *Oubaitori* is simple: don't focus on what you lack, but rather celebrate all the things you have in abundance — your strengths and your abilities. This will help you live a life that's free of the anxiety and self-doubt of the comparison trap. Also, every time you catch yourself comparing, focus on loving everyone around you, and remember that everyone has their own battles they are facing."

Nakoma nodded, grateful for Akira's wisdom.

CHAPTER 28

Fairy Tales

Los Angeles, California.

"I have to say… it doesn't look like much."

Jonathan couldn't help saying it out loud: the gym they were walking through looked like it hadn't been repaired in at least thirty years (if it ever had). The plaster was cracked, the paint was peeling off the walls, and the gym's wood floors had lost their finish years ago. The whole place looked like time itself had moved on, leaving this entire building — and anything inside it — to decay and fall apart. The fact that it was connected to a homeless shelter probably didn't help.

"Oh, we aren't even to the good part yet!" Akira smiled as he looked around.

Jonathan noticed a bounce in the old man's step, as if this dilapidated building energized him somehow. He'd told them that it was incredibly important, but hadn't shared why yet, despite insisting they drive straight here after landing. After all the travel, Jonathan was short on sleep — and patience.

"Well, can we get to 'the good part' so we can see what it is? Or at least… move on to somewhere cleaner?" Jonathan asked, as he sneezed from all the dust and mold.

Akira just smiled wider, ignoring Jonathan's tone. "Right this way."

He led them both across the gym floor, with its creaking boards and fading paint, to a small door that he opened carefully — as if this were holy ground. He was clearly emotional, slowly pulling the door open to reveal a small unlit box of a room. In the shadows they glimpsed deflated basketballs, piles of laundry, and a collection of rusting gym equipment. Dumbbells, a few exercise bikes, even an old Soviet-era rowing machine. The room was like a graveyard.

"The switch should be right there…" Akira pointed to the wall. Sure enough, Nakoma found a few light switches. A cracked fluorescent tube buzzed on overhead, illuminating the space. It somehow looked even smaller once it was lit.

"Akira, what is this place?" Jonathan asked. Despite his frustration, he was certain his old sensei didn't bring them here just to look at some old gym equipment.

"This," Akira replied, "Is where I was living, the day everything changed."

Silence fell for a moment, until Nakoma couldn't resist asking: "Wait… you *lived* here? Like, here in this room?"

Akira nodded, memories flooding over him. "Yes, and it was my choice! I could have lived with a host family the organization would have set me up with, but I wanted to live here. A question I love to ask people is, 'Are you willing to sacrifice, and be faithful to the small things when your dreams are so far off that they feel like fairy tales?'

One day a few months into living and working here, some of the initial inspiration and newness had worn off. I knew that I could help some of the best athletes in the world, yet all I had were three boys, Eric, Jayson, and Bobby.

I got so frustrated one day that I screamed at the top of my lungs and it reverberated off the empty gym walls! **"Why do I only have these three little kids?!"**

That is when I felt like I got punched in the gut with: *Until you value those three little kids like the best in the world, you will NEVER work with people at that level.*

Mother Teresa said, 'Be faithful in the small things, for it is in the small things that your strength lies.' I call that day in this gym the day that everything changed for me, because it was the day I stopped worrying about the size of the opportunity in my hands. Instead, I became obsessed with valuing every opportunity as if it were the biggest in the world.

It is so easy to complain and bemoan what little we have. What is incredibly hard is to be relentless in our faithfulness to that which we *do* have. If you learn to operate from that heart posture of gratitude and ridiculous faithfulness, you cannot help but to attract amazing opportunities.

I used to read the proverb, 'Do you see any truly competent workers? They will serve kings rather than mere men.' I would think, just 'competent' workers? That is a pretty low bar! But think about it. How often do you run into someone who, regardless of their current station in life, pursues their work with exuberant joy and ridiculous faithfulness? At best, I see maybe a few people a year who fall into this category. I always do what I can to see what their dream is, and how I can help. Because thanks to living in this very room, I know what it's like to pursue your dream faithfully, even when it feels as far off as a fairy tale."

CHAPTER 29

Made With Love

San Diego, California.

The train ride from Los Angeles to San Diego was one of Akira's favorite train rides in the world. It was even more special with Nakoma beside him as they saw the sunset over the Pacific Ocean.

Later that evening, they were excited for dinner at a Michelin-starred restaurant.

"I don't understand," Jonathan told the Maitre'd. "It looks like there are plenty of open tables. Am I missing something?" He and Nakoma loved visiting restaurants on the Michelin Guide. Ever since his wife's passing, neither of them had enjoyed cooking all that much.

The Maitre'd adjusted his tie, "I'm sorry, sir. It's against policy to seat patrons before their reservations. We can't accommodate you in the dining area for another twenty minutes, but you can have a seat at the bar."

Confused, Jonathan peered past him into the dining area. "Why? There are at least seven tables available right now. I realize we're 20 minutes ahead of schedule, but I don't understand why you can't just seat us."

"Again, sir, it's our policy. The bar is right this way."

Jonathan opened his mouth, about to say something he'd probably regret, when Akira interjected, giving the man a warm smile. "The bar is fine. Thank you."

He calmly led Jonathan and Nakoma over to the bar, where they ordered their drinks. As they waited, Jonathan got more and more frustrated as the minutes ticked by and the tables in the dining room remained open. While Akira noticed it, he remained calm.

When the drinks came, Jonathan was about to — again — say something he might have regretted, but again Akira interjected. "We'll take the check, please."

The bartender seemed confused, as did Nakoma. "Aren't we eating here?"

"Not tonight," Akira replied simply. "I have somewhere better in mind."

* * *

Fifteen minutes later they walked into a restaurant in North Park. Akira smiled at the host. "Is Flavio here?" Before the host could answer, he saw the man in question — a skinny Italian man with an unmistakable haircut.

"My friends!" Flavio beamed, "Welcome to Siamo Napoli!" He greeted Akira with a huge bear hug. "It has been too long my friend! Last time I saw you it was at my old spot Civico in Little Italy. How did you know where to find me?!"

Akira grinned, "Nakoma here has been teaching me how to use my phone a little better, and I knew a master craftsman like you couldn't retire — *even if* he sold his business and could afford to. I knew if I looked hard enough, I would find you. When I looked at the menu here and saw 'squash blossoms,' I called. The host told me you were the owner, and that the family recipe for those heavenly appetizers was thankfully still being made!"

Flavio beamed; his pride evident. He was in Siamo Napoli every day that it was open chatting with customers and directing the orchestra that is a restaurant. He was in the kitchen many afternoons preparing the night's food as well. The difference in customer service from the previous spot was tangible.

It was so obvious, in fact, that Nakoma's incredulity forced her to speak up, "Flavio, why do you think that other restaurant's staff was so rude and unaccommodating?"

He loved her bluntness, "It is a hard lesson to learn. Sometimes people try so hard to be cool, or look or feel important, that they forget the two most important rules in this business: *Make the customers feel like they are kings and queens, and make the food with love.*

They are trying too hard, but in the wrong ways. Many of these restaurants are also not family owned and family run. This food and this place are my family legacy. My Great Grandma's recipes, that is my brother, and over there is my cousin. This is not just some business. Our family name is on the line. We take that very seriously, and every customer is treated with the same love we make our food with."

"Speaking of which," Jonathan interjected. "I'd love to taste what the fuss is about!"

* * *

113

It turned out, Akira's taste was as dead-on as his aim with a bow. Two hours later, they were stuffed. Nakoma and Jonathan had never tasted such incredible sauces, and the handmade pastas were to die for.

When they finally finished, Jonathan asked for the check. But instead, the waiter came back with a Tiramisu and a piping hot Margherita pizza. Jonathan was confused, "I'm sorry, but we didn't order this. You must have the wrong table."

Hearing this, Flavio came over with a big smile. "Ahh, we got the right table! Akira isn't leaving my restaurant without his desserts! They are on the house."

Akira's face was flushed. When he spoke, he choked up. "You remembered."

Flavio was beaming, "How could I forget, old friend?!"

Akira blinked back tears, knowing this was more than likely the last meal he'd ever taste from his good friend. Flavio didn't know, but Jonathan filled him in. They all shared a big teary group hug, and then scarfed down the rest of the food, full to bursting.

Akira got up and gave Flavio a long hug, thanking him one last time for his gift. "Thank you for showing the world what it looks like to pursue your craft with excellence, and to treat customers like favorite family members rather than just numbers."

CHAPTER 30

"You are an artist"

Mammoth, California.

It was a short one hour flight up to the small airport, but it was always a wild landing in the wind tunnel created by the valley between the mammoth mountains that bore that name. A couple hours later they were up on the slopes with Nakoma's team.

Nakoma crouched as she shot into the halfpipe, momentum slingshotting her across the hard-packed snow. Speed building, she hit the lip with an explosion of motion — rotating three times for a picture-perfect 1080 — before stomping the landing. As she coasted up the other side, she heard Akira cheering nearby…

"Another one!" The old man hadn't stopped smiling all afternoon, and for good reason. He perched at the bottom of the halfpipe, enjoying his front-row seat to Nakoma's practice runs. All day, she'd been putting on a show — nailing trick after trick.

Still, she hadn't yet been able to land the elusive backside 900. After a few attempts, she began to lose focus, so Jonathan encouraged her to do an hour of "fun runs."

Sure enough, an hour later she felt a hundred times better. With all their recent travel, it had been a few weeks since she'd been able to ride, and it was clear her body, mind, and soul had missed it. She unleashed trick after trick — sometimes just enjoying the feeling of grabbing monster air on such a beautiful mountain. By the end of the session, she'd forgotten all about wiping out on so many backside 900s.

Akira could tell, "Kiddo, I don't know anything about snowboarding, but I know a lot about mastery. They are trying to make you into something you aren't. When you do these 'free runs' as you call them, you float like a butterfly and move as gracefully as a snow leopard. You are art embodied in movement. When you do these choreographed runs, you lack all that magic and grace. Don't get me wrong, it's still beautiful and I get why your team wants you to do them. I just think they might be inadvertently taming the fire that burns deep in you."

Nakoma nodded, "Funny you should say that. My team is the best in the world, but one of the first things my new coach told me was that I needed to tamp down the fire and do these runs that are more traditional. He said the judges at the Olympics and X Games don't reward my style."

Akira let out a huge sigh. "So many of these 'experts' project their own insecurities and fears on those they lead. My sensei taught me 'We must master the rules, so when the time is right, we can break them.' The rules are like guide rails, they help you at first, but eventually if you want to fulfill your potential in any craft, especially art, you will have to break them."

"Art?" Nakoma shook her head timidly, looking down. "I just snowboard, I'm not an artist."

Akira grabbed her face gently with both hands, looking directly into her eyes. "THAT, my dear… is the lie they want you to believe. YOU are an artist. THAT is what makes you special and different. You make art on that mountain. Art isn't something reserved for some chosen few that can draw or paint. We are ALL artists at heart. We are born to create, but the systems of society will do everything they can to beat that creativity, originality, and uniqueness out of you. They want to mold you into worker bee drones that do exactly what they are told, and then keep you trapped and drugged up in the pursuit of consumption. We are born to create, but a world full of creators instead of consumers is a radically different world than we live in today. The powers at be don't want that, so that's why we have to fight every day not to fall into their traps and conditioning!"

Nakoma nodded, noticing that Akira had nearly worked himself into a sweat with his passion. She grinned, "Did anyone ever tell you that you should speak with more conviction and emotion?" They both laughed. "I know it's a lot for someone your age, but I hate seeing what the system and well-intentioned people do every day to young people like you."

Nakoma got a big smile on her face. "I know you're right. No one has ever called me an artist, but when you say it, it hits me in my soul. I know that's what I am."

"Yes," Akira agreed, "You are. And that doesn't just apply to snowboarding either. It applies to everything in life.

My whole life people told me I couldn't do things, that I was doing things wrong, that I wasn't an artist, that I was too young, then I was too old… that I'm crazy. Crazy is the word they use to demonize things they don't understand and a mechanism for trying to keep people stuck in places they don't belong. A friend of mine* once said, 'It's dismissive to call these people crazy, these people aren't crazy, maybe their environment is a little sick…at first it is a little scary when they call you crazy, but then it is liberating.'

117

It used to bother me, but now I realize the more uncomfortable my choices make others, the closer I probably am to doing what I'm supposed to be doing.

When you aren't afraid of the pain, the work, or the sacrifice that most people are scared to death of, that is when you open yourself up to wild possibilities in life.

When you are secure in who you are…
When you don't need the approval of others…
When you aren't afraid of being wrong…
When you aren't afraid of looking stupid….
When you trust your gut…
When you do the work in the dark…
When you are willing to take the roads less traveled….
When you are relentless in the pursuit of what sets your soul on fire…

You are going to scare most people to death.

Looking backwards people will be inspired, but in the moment, people will scream and tell you not to do it.

Part of their fear is legitimate care and concern for you, but part of it is that when you do it, you take away all their excuses for living a life of (perceived) safety and mediocrity. You pull back the curtain and show that a lot of what they believed and were conditioned to believe isn't real. That is some scary stuff for them.

The choice is ours at each moment we are gifted.

I hope my life has inspired you that at each opportunity, you choose to dance with the fear rather than run from it. I hope you choose to run towards the hard rather than from it. I hope you choose to live life on your terms rather than the consumerism BS that our entire culture has been conditioned to chase. The sacrifices and work are real, but so are the chains the system has slowly tricked you into wearing.

There is a whole other life possible, and I hope you choose to dance with the fear, sacrifice, and work required, because that is where that other life is.

You are the weapon, Nakoma.
You weren't born for this, like people say.
You were *built* for it."

Nakoma quietly absorbed Akira's words, moved. She knew they had made the right choice to spend all this time with Akira instead of staying back to train.

*Dave Chappelle quote from an interview.

CHAPTER 31

"The magic is inside you"

Jonathan woke up early, with a strange feeling in his chest.

His mentor had slowed down over the past several days while Nakoma trained with her team, his headaches intensifying, and their recovery taking longer. He was sleeping more and speaking less. Jonathan had gotten used to waking up to the smell of fresh coffee no matter what time zone or spot in the world they were at, but today the coffee machine sat there cold and empty. Jonathan brewed a pot, then brought a cup to Akira's room and knocked. A moment later, he heard…

"Come in." Akira's voice was weaker. Softer.

Jonathan entered, heavy with the realization that their time with Akira was nearing an end. He offered him the coffee, noticing how papery-thin and pale Akira's skin looked. His fingers shook, barely able to grasp the cup. Jonathan helped lift it to his lips, letting Akira slowly sip it.

His old sensei noticed him staring, and a small smile lit his face. "Don't worry, I am ready to go home. Remember, from dust we come and to dust we all return. This body, is just a rental."

Jonathan couldn't help laughing. Even now, in the face of death, Akira was absolutely fearless. In fact, his physical strength might be gone, but his spirit seemed even lighter than normal.

"You know, people act like death is contagious. It isn't. Yet most will do anything they can to avoid facing it. They refuse to make peace with death. But in so doing, they make it impossible to make peace with life. When most people hear the phrase 'finish empty' they immediately think of doing more, achieving more… success… performance, and possibly even some overweight coach yelling at them to 'Touch every line.'

While some of that may apply, finishing empty the way I have taught you is about putting first things first and emptying the tank every day in ways that line up with our priorities and who we want to be. All so that, in the end looking back, we might have the peace that comes from knowing we did not compromise on what actually matters.

True contentment comes from knowing we left it all out there and did not sacrifice what truly matters at the altar of what feels important in the moment. At times that may increase short term failure, but what it will greatly increase is the long game satisfaction and contentment of knowing you emptied the tank in the ways that matter most."

* * *

Jonathan spent the next few hours at his mentor's side, joined by Nakoma.

She could sense the inevitable, but it didn't rattle her. Instead, she snuggled up in bed with him. Jonathan was overwhelmed with pride at his daughter's bravery.

They laughed together for hours, sharing embarrassing stories and memories of their time together. Eventually, Jonathan could tell that Akira was fading. The energy went out of his words, and he asked Nakoma to play some of his favorite music as he rested.

A few hours later, as the sun began to set outside and the light shifted across the ceiling, he woke slowly. His eyes were clear, his words calm. "Headache's gone, finally."

Nakoma nodded, then asked, "Can I get you anything?"

Akira shook his head. "No sweetheart, thank you. I have lived most of my life from this perspective, and now that it is here, I have peace. I'm just grateful you are both here with me.

I truly lived while I was alive.
I have no regrets, only gratitude.
I can go freely now, knowing I finished empty."

Nakoma and Jonathan let their tears flow. But they were tears of joy, and awe. They were in awe at the way this little man had lived and loved with his time on this planet. His face practically shone in these final moments.

And then, for a brief moment, a shot of energy seemed to surge through him. He got an intense look on his face and he told her, *"Just remember: No matter what anyone ever says or writes about you, the magic is inside of you, so it can never leave you!"*

Nakoma was really crying now and squeezed him as tight as she could.

After their moment, Akira settled back into bed, his chest rising and falling peacefully now. He grasped Jonathan's hand with one last smile. "I can see my sweet wife. She is calling me home. She looks just as beautiful as the day we first met."

With those final words, Nakoma kissed his head and they stayed with him as he closed his eyes for the final time and eventually, took his last breath.

CHAPTER 32

Celebration of Life

Akira's funeral was more like a massive party. Everyone was dressed to the nines, at Akira's request. He wanted everyone to show up and show out in honor of him, rather than be there to morn him. Jonathan and Nakoma looked spectacular in their bespoke ISAIA suits.

Visitors from around the world, from every level of society and every professional field were in attendance. World leaders, businessmen, athletes, more than a few celebrities. Former students, hundreds of them.

There was so much laughter mixed with the tears and memories. And food — so much food. Somehow, Flavio had seemed to transplant his entire restaurant on site, working tirelessly as trays of Akira's favorite dishes were passed through the crowd.

Looking around, Jonathan couldn't help but smile. It was exactly what Akira had told them — his real "life's work" was the people he had been blessed to do life with.

* * *

Through the afternoon, many people shared stories about the impact Akira had on their lives, and the final speaker was now at the podium.

"It wasn't long after I took the position as head of global sales for United Airlines that I heard people mention Sensei Akira's name as a person that I must meet. He was hesitant about me at first, unsure about my 'positivity,' as he called it. You all know he was no fan of positivity."

Everyone chuckled, as Dave Hilfman went on, "We became fast friends when he finally understood what was behind my outlook on life. We both lost our wives at ages that were cruel at best. As he initially did, people sometimes mistake my optimism and joy for life as 'positivity.' But it is much deeper than that.

You see, my Tracey, she was so young when she got diagnosed. We had a seven-year old boy, Marshall. We had a beautiful life, and then in a moment's notice it was flipped upside down. Every day, while she fought things and a pain I could never understand, she did it with a smile and courage I couldn't help but be inspired by.

She wanted to live so badly. She would have given anything for more time on this planet even as cancer ravaged her body. I made her a promise, *'I will never have a bad day. I will live every single day and spin I get on this planet to the fullest. I will live, laugh, and love with every fiber of my being. I know how bad you want to be here, and I will live for both of us.'*

So for me, there's no such thing as a bad day, because she would give anything for my worst day here…

I learned so much from Akira-Sensei, but one of my most special memories was the day he told me how much my perspective and choice to 'finish empty' had impacted him. It brought me to tears when I got the handwritten note from him a few months ago asking me to speak when this day inevitably came.

I hope that we will use his incredible life as a reminder to *always love, live, and be with everything we have.*"

* * *

Afterward, Jonathan and Nakoma sat together out on the porch, watching the sun set.

Finally, Jonathan stirred, "You know, he wanted you to have this."

He gave her a sealed letter with her name on it. But before she could open the envelope, an alarm sounded on both of their phones. They checked it, a reminder that their flight for the X Games left early the next day. With everything going on, they'd almost forgotten.

Jonathan looked over at Nakoma, his voice gentle with understanding: "You know, we don't have to go. There's always next year."

For a long moment, Nakoma was quiet. When she finally stirred and looked up, her eyes were filled with determination. "Next year isn't promised. Like Akira taught us: there's only the present. I am blessed with the opportunity to compete, so I will."

Jonathan nodded, a smile growing. Of the many qualities he loved that his daughter possessed, her competitive fire was perhaps his favorite.

CHAPTER 33

Winter X Games

Niseko, Japan.

Nakoma had competed in countless big snowboarding competitions, but this was a very different stage. She'd never seen a mountain packed with this many people.

Crowds of fans filed through security checkpoints and mobbed the slopes. Wherever she looked, sponsorship logos covered huge tents, their flags flapping in the icy wind. Media trucks from multiple networks from around the world were everywhere, and the mountain was lit up like daylight under the massive banks of floodlights. Cameras tracked every run as the announcers' voices boomed from huge loudspeakers.

Nakoma's heart pounded in her chest as she arrived, nerves blaring. She felt so small. The best riders in the world were here, athletes she had looked up to since she could first ride. And the cameras — they were everywhere, like little black eyes looking right at her. After the incident, she couldn't help but feel like she was under a microscope. Media had been hounding her with questions and they didn't appreciate that she would just smile and stay silent when they asked about it. Jonathan taught her very early in life that she didn't owe anyone an answer just because they wanted to know something, especially when it was personal. He knew she would face unfair questions, and that "Even a fool is counted as wise when he keeps his mouth shut."

Jonathan noticed her growing unease, putting a gentle hand on hers. He guided them through the final check-in and rode the lift up to the top of the mountain with her. As they waited for her first run, he didn't say a word. He didn't need to. He'd memorized his daughter's pre-run routine by now, knowing that she was visualizing each movement of her run as she listened to her trigger songs.

And then she was up. She paused her music for a moment, bumping fists with Jonathan, who reminded her: "Just another mountain."

She nodded, took a deep breath, and hit 'play'. As the beat dropped, so did she, gliding down the mountain into her first run.

While she landed everything, her legs never felt right — refusing to fully obey her mind as she spun, flipped, and launched her way across the half-pipe. On her final trick, she lost speed coming off the wall, and what was supposed to be a massive 1080 ended up as a much-tamer 720, with a shaky landing.

Despite a burst of applause, Nakoma was frustrated.

This was good, but nothing compared to what she had in her. As the youngest competitor, she knew no one expected her to place, much less win — and the run she'd just put together was respectable for her age. But she also knew that a 720 wasn't big enough to win, not here. This wasn't some regional comp, it was the Winter X Games. The judges wouldn't score her better just for being younger. This was the big leagues.

Sure enough, her score showed it: good, not great. In fact, it reflected exactly how she felt about her run: stiff and awkward. Still, it was enough to put her in the top 6 riders. She could reach the winner's podium, but it would take a monster run to get there.

"We came, so might as well let it fly." Before her next run, Jonathan smiled and winked at her as she prepared to head into the pipe again.

And let it fly she did. At least, she tried. But still, her landings were sloppy, her edge never felt clean — and as she went into her final trick, something happened that rarely did. She lost power in the air, under-rotated, and nearly wiped out, hand dropping down instinctively to stabilize her — a move she knew would cost her.

She stared at her score for a long moment — "8.1" — and realized then that she was out, dropping all the way down to 9th place. She would have to deliver a flawless run to overtake the leader. It had never been done, and she knew it... she couldn't beat this.

She slammed her board in frustration, her head erupting like a bursting firehose of negative thoughts — each one louder than the last.

You don't belong...
They were all right about you...
What did you think would happen when you took so many weeks off?
You're not a pro... Look at all these other riders, they're all better than you.
Give up. No one expects you to win...
What were you thinking? You look like an idiot out here...
Everyone knows you don't belong...

Her vision blurring, chest pounding with each frantic, hammering heartbeat, Nakoma walked numbly to the competitor rest area and collapsed into the snow. All sound seemed to drop away, as a wave of raw fear overwhelmed her. Then, through the fog of overwhelm, she heard her father's voice…

"Hey kiddo, I'm with you."

Jonathan sat beside her, not saying anything more. He didn't have to. His presence alone helped calm and reassure her. The silence stretched for a while, until he asked the question she didn't have an answer for just yet…

"We only have a few minutes to let them know if you're going to drop. Do you want to keep going?"

For the first time in her life, Nakoma knew she didn't.

CHAPTER 34

Finish Empty

As Nakoma stood up, ready to tell Jonathan that she was going to drop, she heard the crinkle of paper inside her jacket. She paused, reaching inside to feel a thin envelope…

Akira's letter.

She felt the edges of the paper, hesitating. She intuitively knew what was inside, and even thinking about the words was enough to shift her resolve. She turned to Jonathan, the competitive fire reignited inside of her. "I *want* to keep going. Even if I fail, I am going to honor Akira by finishing empty."

Jonathan just nodded, a surge of pride behind his smile. "I'll let them know."

* * *

As Nakoma and Jonathan rode the lift back up the mountain toward the halfpipe, she opened Akira's letter. The roar of the crowd, the booming voices of the announcers, the pounding music… all of it faded away as she read his words:

Nakoma,

There is an ancient secret that has been quietly passed down for thousands of years, but that has been all but forgotten in our modern world.

The journey is a precious and quickly passing gift.

We are so caught up in the maze of achievement and accolades that we have lost sight of the true prize.

The philosopher Epictetus said, "No great thing is created suddenly." It is important to remember that the journey of earning something is what allows us the grit, wisdom, and stamina needed to maintain it.

In today's society, where instant gratification is not only put on a pedestal, but also a fervent desire and increasing baseline expectation, it's easy to forget that only in the struggle can strength and stamina be developed. The hardest challenges are an opportunity for special.

What you achieve in any moment is not nearly as important as who you become in the process.

By embracing the challenges and difficulties that come along the journey, you'll develop the character and fortitude necessary to maintain and grow, rather than achieve then flounder.

Do not shy away from the struggles and pressure but instead embrace them with open arms, knowing they are the stepping stones and forging ground for sustained excellence.

There are many roads and shortcuts to cheap wins and accolades, but there is only one path to sustained excellence. It takes what it takes.

There is a day quickly coming when you will desperately wish for one more chance at the thing you are now despising. Those on their death bed know this all too well. Those whose bodies are ravaged with cancer look out and see people everywhere doing all sorts of hard and painful things, things they would love to do, but can't anymore.

We get glimpses of this reality throughout our life. When we lose a loved one, and we yearn for them to do that silly or annoying thing, just one more time. When we get injured and we yearn for the opportunity to do the thing we hated just days and weeks before. When a relationship disintegrates, and we yearn for one last night to hold them instead of sleeping on the couch in anger.

Do it while you can.
Treasure every moment.
Savor every kiss.
Soak in every ounce of pain.
Learn to love it all.

Because as sure as the sun will set in the west, there is a day coming where you will long for one more at bat in life..... but we only get one.

So let's finish empty.
Let's find the joy in this moment.
Let's love the struggle.

Even in the pain of today, let's love where we are.

The challenges will be the same, but with a new perspective we can find fresh wind for our sails.

Love the shit out of the hard, the painful, the loss, because only those who know the depths of that can experience the beauty of the opposite. It's the contrast that makes the difference. Without the negative, we can't truly appreciate the positive. Without lack we don't really understand abundance. Without tragedy, we can't truly appreciate triumph.

Be exactly who you know in your gut you were created to be.
Do not dim your flame to make weak people comfortable.
Be one of the very few who at the end of their life had the courage to live the way they were meant to live, instead of having the number one regret of the dying.

Excuses are sweet music to our damaged egos that want to throw in the towel, but they are a poisonous, slow death to our potential. For every legitimate excuse there are more pathways of possibility.

Push through the pain.
Smile at the hard.

Keep getting back up, even when you've been knocked down so many times no one would blame you for quitting.

Legends are built when ordinary people smile and run towards what most people run from. Small choices, added up, and compounded over time. There's no extraordinary people. Our heroes are just ordinary people, willing to consistently make extraordinary choices.

Pressure is <u>THE</u> privilege.
Embrace it fully.
Love it all.
Finish empty.

Love you kiddo.

-Sensei Akira

Wiping away a freezing tear, Nakoma took a deep breath and looked at Jonathan. They now stood by the starting gate, a huge clock showing three minutes before her final run.

She took a deep breath, the emotion and pressure giving way to a newfound clarity freed up within her by Akira's words.

"Dad, I read more about that David guy. The King had given him his personal armor to wear, but David went out to face Goliath with no armor. I appreciate all the time my team has spent with me trying to choreograph a 'winning run.' But you know I didn't start snowboarding to win medals. I used to snowboard because it's what I loved, and it allowed me to make art on the mountain. All the trophies are just a byproduct of my love of the game.

Like Akira taught me, life is a single player game. No one is riding on this mountain with me, and I've listened to far too much outside feedback and advice. It's time for me to go back to my heart, and board the way only I was built to board. I'm taking radical responsibility so I can have radical acceptance of whatever happens.

It's just another mountain, and it's time I just make art on it.

I'm tired of listening to all the outside noise. I'm tired of trying to be who everyone else wants me to be. I'm tired of hearing 'You can't do it that way', 'This is a different league.' Great! If being myself and doing what I love isn't good enough to compete, I can live with that. What I can't live with, especially in light of Akira's life and death, is not living life on my terms. I've always known, and he confirmed it in his final moments: *the magic is inside of me.* It's time to go make magic, my way."

She looked down at her jacket and pants — bulky, covered with colorful sponsor logos — and then took them off, stripping down to her lighter underlayer. This was how she'd always boarded when she was younger, preferring the freedom of movement it gave her to tear up the mountain. It felt perfect for this final run.

Jonathan smiled, impressed by her boldness. "I know how excited you were to get all those big sponsor deals. You know they won't be happy."

As Nakoma slipped her competitor bib back on, the familiar fire was back in her eyes. "I know. But this run isn't for them. It's for me and Akira."

Jonathan nodded, as the signal sounded for Nakoma to get into position. In the chute, she closed her eyes and visualized a huge ball of unconditional love. Then — as she had practiced many times — she stepped into the ball and let everything else melt away.

She no longer worried about failure. All she cared about was operating out of love and being fully present in the moment. Internally, she released any expectation for what would come next. She pushed any thought about her routine — which tricks to land, in which order — out of her mind, surrendering the outcome. The point of life wasn't to arrive safely at death. This life was hers — a single player game — the controller was in her hands.

Just before she gave the signal to the gate operator, she whispered, "*Remember who you are. It's time to be an artist.*" When the gate opened, she shot down the mountain, attacking the half-pipe with the freedom and unbridled courage she had when she first started boarding.

The moment she exploded off the pipe and into the air, *everyone* knew this run was different.

But Nakoma wasn't thinking about it — *in fact, she wasn't thinking at all*. She didn't have to. Her body and soul were simply dancing across the mountain the way she danced in the rain. She didn't think — or care — about which trick came next. Everything flowed out of her, pure instinct, artistry in motion. She was operating in a pure flow state.

The crowd couldn't believe what they were witnessing. They all knew this was special, and history in the making. At the end of her run, she crouched into the wall of the half-pipe, and shot off it with more speed than she'd ever felt heading into a jump — exploding off the lip of the pipe, she flipped and turned in a way no one had ever seen. The trick she landed seemed to defy gravity and physics, and to top it off, she gracefully landed as soft as a butterfly.

In every media booth, announcers buzzed about Nakoma — the 13-year-old who had just shocked the world with a final run that blew everyone away. And when her scores lit up the board a minute later, the roar of applause and pure energy crashed over the entire mountain like a tsunami.

Nakoma stared, stunned — a perfect "10.0" — *she had just won the gold medal*. Not by landing a backside 900. Not by performing or executing a perfect plan. She did it by surrendering the outcome, trusting her training, and being one with her body and the mountain.

Jonathan burst through the crowd, tackling her with a bear hug into the snow. They could barely contain their joy, its intensity mingling with the deep ache of sorrow that came from knowing that while this victory was theirs, it also belonged to a man who was no longer with them.

Nakoma smiled through her tears, "He was with me, Dad. He was with me!"

Jonathan grinned back, pride radiating. "I know, honey. We all saw it. It was one of the most beautiful things I've ever seen."

* * *

Later that night, an airplane took off from Tokyo, beginning its long journey back across the Pacific. Alone in his seat, Jonathan watched as Nakoma slept nearby. Her gold medal was stuffed away in her bag, but in her hand, she still held the letter she'd received from Akira. She had fallen asleep reading it again and again.

He looked over at the empty seat next to him. Without Akira in it, it seemed so strange after all their travels together. But then he took a deep breath, realizing — he wasn't truly alone. Akira would always be with them. His lessons and the memories they made together had been woven so deeply into Jonathan's life that he knew he could never forget them.

He opened Akira's journal, or *"manuscript"*, as he had called it.

It was blank. Page by page, Jonathan flipped through it and couldn't find anything. He started to panic a little, wondering if he'd gotten the wrong one. But then he reached the very last page.

It was there he found a simple note.

Jonathan,

We've already lived the book,
just tell them the story.

P.S. Nakoma's voice and perspective will
be very important for this book.

Love You,

Sensei Akira

Jonathan couldn't help but laugh at his wily mentor. He had always told Jonathan he hated writing, and preferred living life in the trenches with people, experimenting with real solutions to real problems rather than sitting in some office theorizing.

Jonathan breathed deeply, shook his head with a smile, "Sure, Akira. I'll chop the wood and carry the water for you one more time, old friend."

Then he opened the notes app in his phone and started typing...

Finish Empty
-What does it look like to live a TRULY successful life
from a death bed perspective?

A note from Joshua.

I consider this story autobiographical fiction. Most of the places, people, and conversations are a mash up from my real life. You may also like to know that the final book in the trilogy will be, *You Are The Weapon*. It will follow the next season in Nakoma and Jonathan's life. While I have most of the story mapped out in my head and in notes on my phone, it will probably be at least a couple of years before we bring it to life. After that, if I still find that I have more to contribute to the world, I could possibly be convinced to write the prequel to *Chop Wood Carry Water*, which is Akira's origin story, *Sharpen The Axe*.

Here are some pictures of me with some of the people from the book.

Joshua with his baby brother Jordan. Jordan drowned a few months after this picture was taken. Joshua was the one who found him in the pool and pulled him out. Jordan was the love of Joshua's young life. He was his best friend, and one of the most incredible kids ever.

Joshua and Tonja after having just seen a double rainbow in Social Circle, GA. Rainbows were Bengie's favorite.

Joshua and Dave Hilfman after a golf tournament victory.

Joshua with his "sister" Jenn Kessler and her family wearing a few of Joshua's faux fur coats. Matt Kessler tells the boys to be "curious and kind" every day before they leave for school. Ciaran (on the left) and Joshua share the same birthday. Jack is on the right. Joshua and Jenn both played sports at Vanderbilt and have called each other brother and sister since freshman year.

Joshua and Julia at the ISAIA store in Capri, Italy.

Joshua at the majestic lake in Iceland.

@jonfromiceland on the first trip when he and Joshua were exploring Iceland. You can follow his adventures on Instagram.

Ben in Chicago with Joshua for a leadership retreat, right after
he gave Joshua his custom timepiece.

World Map with the darker areas closer to the actual scale of
size.

Flavio holding one of Joshua's favorite margarita pizzas.

Additional T2BC Resources

We are a heart centered approach to leadership and mental training whose focus is equipping people to put first things first, and live life through a death lens perspective. We focus on helping people make love and courage their dominating operating system instead of fear and shame.

Occasionally, we help people perform better as well!

Keynote Speaking- email joshua@traintobeclutch.com

Mentorship Program- Our mentorship program isn't a good fit for everyone, but we are always willing to see if it is a good fit for you. It is a serious investment of time and resources. Email amber@traintobeclutch.com for more information.

T2BC Reading Challenge- email amber@traintobeclutch.com for a free copy

Books- For a custom bulk discount email amber@traintobeclutch.com and she will get you setup. Bulk orders take a minimum of three weeks from the time we receive payment.

Our books are available on Amazon, Kindle, and Audible.

Other books by Joshua Medcalf. In order of publishing dates.

Burn Your Goals.
Transformational Leadership.
Chop Wood Carry Water.
Hustle.
Pound The Stone.
The Future of Leadership.
Win In The Dark.
Dear Future Mrs. President.
From Hack To Scratch.

YouTube- Our channel is *train2bclutch*
Twitter- @joshuamedcalf
Instagram- @realjoshuamedcalf
Website- t2bc.com
Cell: 918-361-8611 *(text is best, but yes, it's me, and I do respond)*

Thank YOU to Jacob Roman. *IF, I could do this without you, it sure would suck. Appreciate all you do to make the stories in my head really come to life.*

Thank YOU to everyone in the launch group for helping make this story better! Andrew Downing, Konnor Beste, Steve Powell, Robyn Straley, Jason Jochimsen, Stu Mendelsohn, Mike Maccaro, Danny Woodall, Mike Connor, Saul Luna, Amy Knoche, Elijah Cope, Joey Slovensky, Tyler Lee, Neil Weiner, Trisha Kroll, Evan Spears, David Mills, Brian Fogt, Jeremiah Davis, David Geier, JT Ayers. Heath Hunter, Blayne Hobbs, Daryl Dotson, John Woods, Dustin Swigart, Duane Vaughn, Robin Bachnik, Angel Elderkin, Jim Collins, Charlie Webb, Tim Miller, Missy Gerst, Jesse Bouchard, Ken Sanford, David Schexnaydre Jr., Tim Haneburg, Triesch Family, Reggie Christiansen, Tim Johnson, Kurtis Jai Mays, Lambert Brown, Paula Bennett, Tim Budge, Chuka Erike, Greg Brown, Reba Quattlebaum, Jared Cecil, Austin Phillips, Rex Stump, Nathan Dmochowski, Greg Gale, Nate Crandall, Jay Fletch, Rob Hammond, Rich Bonn, Shane O'Brien, Maria Chininis, Jon Pereiro, Brad Pederson, Shelly Hotzler, Tina Beauvais, James Metz, Tammy Yaw, Daniel Meadows, Andrew Webster, Michael Meadow, Mike Medici, Austin Butler, Tommy Hulihan

Made in United States
Orlando, FL
09 July 2024

48777657R00093